DIANNE OREN

Happily Ever After in the Hollow

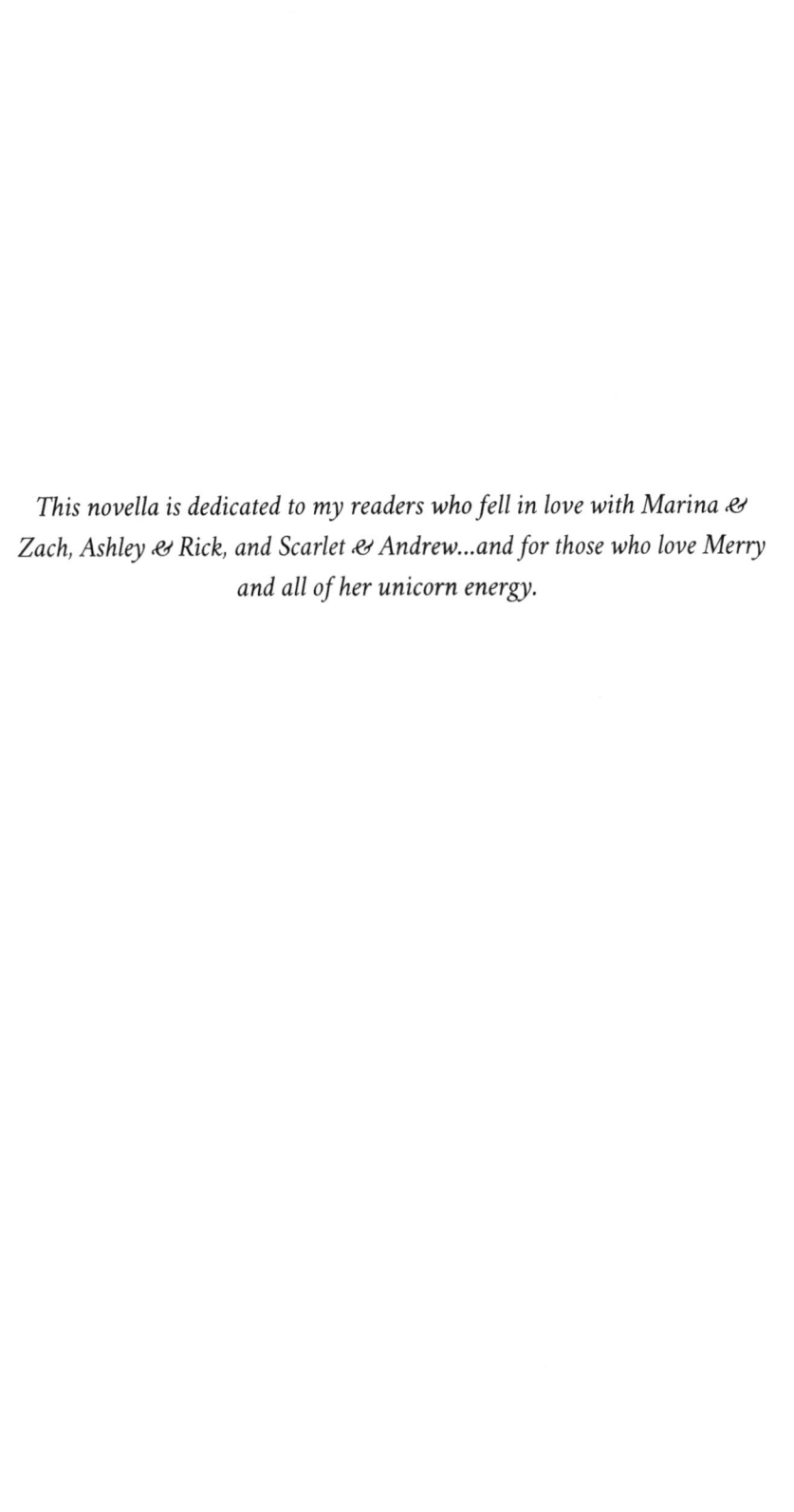

This novella is dedicated to my readers who fell in love with Marina &
Zach, Ashley & Rick, and Scarlet & Andrew...and for those who love Merry
and all of her unicorn energy.

Contents

Acknowledgments

Y'all...again, thank you. If you're reading this novella, if you've read my other books...if you've pre-ordered Merry & Bright...thank you. You are the reason I'm living this dream and I'm forever grateful.

To my husband and my crazy family...thank you for backing me up and believing in me.

I have to say thank you so, so much to my beta team...The Horsemen. :-) We change their group name with every book I write, so they got to be headless for this one. Thank you so much for all the reading you do and the feedback you give. I couldn't do this without you.

To my ARC team...OMG thanks for your help with another one! Thanks for reading and reviewing and helping me bring my books to print/digital. You're amazing.

And to my friends...I love you. Thanks for cheering me on, in whatever way you've done it. Thanks for loving me exactly as I am.

Finally...to Washington Irving, for writing the most wonderful short story "The Legend of Sleepy Hollow". My nine-year-old heart fell in love with this story and I've never been the same.

Content Warnings

This is a sweet romantic comedy with kissing only, no spice, and a guaranteed happy ending. No one gets sick, no one dies. That said, I want readers to feel like they're safe...so here are some things to consider:

There is a child in foster care who is being bullied at school, which is talked about by some of the characters. Another character is on crutches because of an injury. There's a chapter that takes place in a pub (no one gets drunk or anything). Some little old ladies may or may not flirt with Rick...but c'mon, so would we. Right?

A note about Sleepy Hollow, New York: the town is very real (and very cool...I highly recommend a visit). While I have described some things about the town that really exist, the businesses and people mentioned in this book are purely from my imagination.

I

Marina & Zach

Chapter 1

Marina

I stand at the kitchen sink, watching the love of my life fussing over a pumpkin vine in the backyard garden, and laugh under my breath. This is all my fault. My husband. My sweet, gorgeous, sexy, rockstar husband is looking for squash bugs, and it's all my fault.

There are times when I think of all that's transpired over the past few years, and I marvel at how this is my life. Whatever the reason, I'm grateful for all of it, including the fact that I'm a born and bred city girl who has no idea how to garden and should definitely not be trusted to care for anything that doesn't have a face. Now, poor Zach has to deal with the result of my ignorance. He's handling it like a champ.

It's actually his fault, anyway. The backyard at our Sleepy Hollow, New York estate is massive, and Zach thought it might be fun for us to start a garden. On the surface, that seemed like a great idea. Until I realized that there are lots of bugs in gardens. That's a big no for me. But my folly doesn't end there. Nope. Zach left me in charge of planting the pumpkins, and I thought it would be great to have three pumpkins amongst the fall decorations on our big wrap-around porch. So I planted three pumpkin seeds, despite not realizing that pumpkins grow on vines. Multiple pumpkins per vine. So now my sweet husband is knee-deep in a field of pumpkin vines, doing what he can, because I checked out the first time I saw a squash bug. At last count, seventeen pumpkins are growing.

Oops.

The muffled sound of footsteps upstairs brings a warm smile to my face. Merry. She flew in from San Francisco last night, arriving early to help me prep for the biggest party Zach and I have thrown since we married. Almost all of our loved ones will be here for it, with many staying in the house or the two guest houses located on the far side of the back lot.

As the resident newlyweds of our group, I've assigned Scarlet and Andrew to one of the guest houses. Rick and Ashley have the other. Everyone else is in the main house with us, and with twelve bedrooms, we're still packed to the gills. Zach and I have been looking forward to this weekend for months, for quite a few reasons. My biggest goal is to help Merry emerge from the emotional funk she's been in.

Merry is the unicorn energy of our group. Fantastically extra in all the best ways, she can make any of us see the light in the darkest of circumstances. She is a beautiful ball of bold energy and kindness, and we're all a little worried about the fact that there's a little less rainbow in our unicorn lately.

"Hey, girl," Merry chirps as she breezes into the kitchen. She immediately homes in on the pink box on the counter. "What's in the box?"

I turn away from the window and pull two coffee mugs from the cabinet. The coffeemaker is gurgling away, filling the kitchen with a wonderful aroma.

"Pumpkin spice donuts, and they're fabulous. Help yourself. I've got bacon in the air fryer. Did you sleep well?"

"So well, I feel like accusing you of putting melatonin powder in my pillow."

I laugh and shake my head, then grab a few napkins from the pantry and put them next to the box of donuts.

I'm feeling a little extra gratitude to Merry right now. She arrived a full day before the rest of our friends to help me with the baking for our weekend Halloween celebration. Because, hey, when you own an estate in the legendary town of Sleepy Hollow, New York, you celebrate Halloween.

Merry sighs dramatically as she plops herself onto a barstool on the other side of our massive kitchen island. She flips the box open and inhales.

"Wow," she groans. "That smells so good it hit my ovaries, dude."

I laugh out loud, then immediately hear the screech of a sneaker against the tile. Zach is frozen in the doorway.

"Are you ladies having girl talk? I can come back."

"It's safe, baby, get in here."

Zach grins at me and steps over to give me another good morning kiss. I'm not sure how many we're up to this morning. Fourteen maybe? After kissing me, he heads straight to Merry, who gets a hug and a very loud, smoochy kiss on the cheek because it always makes her laugh. He grabs a seat at the island as well, and I grab the creamer jug and sugar bowl, setting them in the middle.

Merry and Zach chatter to themselves while I head into the dining room and look through the china cabinet for the gift I picked up for Zach. I carefully pull the teacup and saucer out and make my way back to the kitchen. He's busy with Merry, so I hit the power button on his electric kettle to flash-boil the water. I grab the carafe of coffee and set it on a trivet on the island for Merry and me. When the water boils, I prepare Zach's favorite breakfast tea in the new teacup and gently place it in front of him, waiting for him to notice.

"I thought it was working out with Jeremy?" Zach says, sounding sincerely disappointed for Merry.

"Nope," she shrugs. "I can't be with a guy who hates sugar. What would we ever talk about?"

Usually, I would argue, but she has a point. Merry is an excellent baker, and her dream is to open her own bakery. Poor Jeremy would never survive it.

"It was that bad?" Zach probes.

Merry smirks. "After I spent six hours baking and frosting a cake order for an anniversary party, Jeremy picked me up for our date and told me I smelled bad."

I purse my lips and pour some coffee into my mug while Zach chuffs, offended on Merry's behalf. He reaches over to pick up the creamer jug and finally notices his teacup.

"What's this?" he gasps as he lifts the teacup for a closer look.

I beam as I watch him admire the black teacup with an intricately painted Headless Horseman galloping around the edge. The saucer is also black, with the words "the horseman comes" painted in gothic white letters. It's the perfect gift for Zach, who has loved the story of Sleepy Hollow and the Headless Horseman since he was just a boy. Zach carefully sets the teacup back on its saucer and stands, coming around the island and pulling me into his arms.

"I love it so much, Siren," he tells me in his sexy British accent that I never tire of hearing. "Wherever did you find it?"

I rub my hand across his back. "In town, if you can believe it. I've never seen it in that shop before, but I guess now that Halloween is here, they're stocking new things for all the tourists."

"I love it," he says sweetly, brushing his lips to mine briefly. "And I love you."

"Mmm...same," I sigh as I watch him sit back down.

He grabs the one and only plain donut I made sure was in the box. He puts it on a napkin for himself, then plucks out a pumpkin spice donut and puts it on a napkin for me. I finish doctoring my coffee and then take a seat between Zach and Merry, taking a bite of my donut and letting out a satisfied groan.

"So good."

Zach's husky laugh sounds throughout the kitchen.

"You Americans and your pumpkin spice."

Merry snorts.

"If you don't like pumpkin spice, you're not gonna like about forty percent of what I bake today."

Zach winks at Merry. "But I'll be sure to enjoy the sixty percent that isn't. And I one hundred percent appreciate you helping my darling Siren, love."

Merry sways her head with a silly grin. The combination of Zach's accent and calling any female "love" usually creates a blush, or a snicker, or...in Merry's case...the head sway. It's adorable.

"Do we not know any single, worthy gentlemen that we can set Merry up with, darling?" Zach asks over his tea.

Merry waves her hands in the air. "Nope! No outside interference, thank you. I appreciate the thought, but no."

Zach tilts his head at her. "You don't like to be set up on dates?"

She shakes her head. "Nope. I think if someone is meant for me, they're going to show up. And they're not going to tell me I stink just because I smell like sugar. And they certainly won't tell me I'll look better as a blonde."

Zach nods. "Here, here! I support that."

Merry bows her head in thanks.

"Seriously, what a creep," Zach says. "You're beautiful just as you are. I'm sorry he was unworthy."

Merry grins. "Are you sure you don't have a twin? I might end my dating hiatus for a twin of yours."

Zach laughs. "Sorry, love."

"Well, whatever his name was, I excused myself to go to the ladies' room and never went back to the table."

Zach holds up his teacup to her. "Cheers, Merry. Well done."

She carefully clinks her mug against his teacup and sips her coffee. The air fryer dings, and I open the door, pulling out several strips of delicious bacon and dropping them on a paper towel. I blot all the grease off before putting the slices on a plate and placing it next to the box of donuts.

Merry takes two pieces, and I offer the plate to Zach, who winks at me.

"That's not bacon, Siren."

I smirk at him. "We are on the west side of the pond, baby. This is bacon."

Zach shoots me his best fake scowl, and I laugh softly, then turn to Merry.

"So what does my favorite baker require today? I can be an extra set of hands."

Merry folds her lips inward as she tries to come up with a reply that isn't a thousand percent honest, so I get ready for a real zinger.

"I've seen what your hands can do in the kitchen," she says with a barely suppressed grin. "Keep those mitts away from me, madam."

I feign shock, holding up my hands and wiggling my fingers. Not like jazz hands...more like *look what these bad boys can do.*

"I'll have you know that these babies can open the finest cans and frozen food boxes the world has to offer."

She shakes her head. "None of those are allowed on my watch. You can go decorate or do other pre-party shenanigans and leave me alone with the flour, sugar, and all the baking goodness."

I smirk at my friend.

"Okay, well, all the ingredients you requested are in the pantry, and I guess I'll waffle around between watching my genius baker friend and doing party stuff."

Merry takes a bite of her donut and nods.

"Deal."

"So what delicacies will you be baking, Merry?" Zach asks as he stirs his tea. "Will there be unicorn cookies from our unicorn friend?"

"Those were not on Marina's request list, sorry," she replies. "But you can enjoy salted caramel cupcakes, freshly made apple pies baked in cute little jars, or maple creme sandwich cookies. I won't mention all the pumpkin spice lovelies I'm baking."

Zach grins at her. "Sounds like I'll be in a proper sugar coma by Sunday. Looking forward to it."

"Just part of the excellent service I provide," Merry beams proudly. "So what else is planned for the weekend?"

I grin excitedly. "I can't wait for you to see how this town celebrates Halloween. We'll go for a walk tomorrow night around sunset. There's an actor who rides a horse dressed as the Headless Horseman. The main street through town looks incredible."

Merry looks incredulous. "Headless? How does he see?"

I laugh and give her a shrug. "I have no idea how it works, but it looks freaking cool."

Merry grins and takes another bite of her donut.

"Tonight is cocktails and dinner," I explain. "Everyone should be here by tonight. Scarlet, Andrew, and Max will get here too late for dinner, but they'll join us for breakfast in the morning."

"She's so busy lately. I'm glad she's able to be here this weekend. I miss her so much."

"She had to work right up until the last minute," Zach chimes in. "There weren't any commercial flights that worked with her schedule, so I'm bringing them over in the Rebels jet."

Merry laughs. "What did we ever do before you fell in love with Marina, dude?"

Zach bolts out of his seat and grabs me, burying his face in my neck and growling dramatically. The combination of his warm breath against my skin and the very sexy growl set me on fire. I hold on for dear life. He kisses me soundly and sits back down with a wicked grin.

"I don't know what I ever did without my Siren, Merry," he says sweetly. "And all of you welcomed me into your lives like it was no big deal, despite the media mess and all that. There isn't anything I wouldn't do for any of you."

Merry gestures at him with the remnants of her donut. "You're good people, Zach. I wish we could clone you so I could just marry Clone Zach."

We both laugh, but I'm a little worried about Merry. She changed her anti-dating policy around the time Scarlet got married, but she's been kissing a lot of frogs and still hasn't met anyone resembling a prince. I want to help her. Hillary's brother is a nice guy, and I'd love to set them up, but she's already told Zach no. I don't want to push it. Still, something's got to give. Merry is the best. I know there's someone out there for her.

My phone vibrates on the counter just as Zach begins pulling his phone from his pocket. If we're getting a text at the same time, I know exactly who it is, and I frantically reach for my phone to check my messages. Merry looks on with undisguised curiosity. I swipe open my phone, then gasp loudly as I jump into Zach's arms with joy.

"What's up, dudes?" Merry asks with a big smile.

Zach gently lets me go and starts typing on his phone.

"I'll reply, love," he says quickly. "You fill Merry in."

I give Zach a quick kiss and turn to Merry.

"There's a girl that I've been working with a lot at the Mermaid Foundation," I begin. "She's had a rough time of things. She's in foster care for now, but she's far from settled. She reminds me of myself a lot after my mom died and Max and I went into foster care."

Merry nods, clearly interested in where this is going.

"Zach and I have both grown close to her. She comes to the office after school so her foster mom can work until five, but she also loves to sing, so Zach and I have been encouraging that as much as we can."

Merry grins. "I like this kid already."

I nod. "Olivia is the sweetest girl. A little rough around the edges because of all she's gone through, but she just needs someone to believe in her. She was afraid to put her name in for her school's talent show, but she just texted us that she did it. It's a huge milestone for her."

Merry sits back in her seat, and her hand flutters up to her heart.

"That is so sweet! How old is she?"

"She's nine," I reply. "A little younger than I was when I entered the foster care system, but just as lost and alone."

Merry shakes her head. "But she's not alone. She has you and Zach. I can't think of two better people to be in her corner."

Zach sits in his seat again and grins at us.

"Well, I told her how proud we are and that we'll do a video chat with her tonight before bed."

Merry smirks at Zach. "You're too perfect, Zach. You need more flaws."

Zach throws his head back and lets out a deep, throaty chuckle.

"Oh, I'm plenty flawed, love. But thank you."

"So what's the foster situation like? Will they adopt her?" Merry asks.

I shake my head. "Sadly, no. This is a single foster parent who isn't interested in adopting, but she is amazing with kids like Olivia, who need consistency and special care."

"Well, with you watching over her, I'm sure she'll end up in a good place," Merry says sweetly.

I run over and give her a quick squeeze around the shoulders.

"Thanks, girl."

"So what are you going to do with yourself now that I've denied your application for sous chef?"

I smirk at my friend.

"We hired extra help to get everything prepared, so I guess I'll head out to the guest cottages to make sure they're all set up, and then I can make sure the bedrooms in the house are ready."

Merry shakes her head in disbelief.

"Seriously, this house is so huge I can't imagine having to deal with having this many people over at once. You're going to be an amazing duchess someday."

"That is just about the sweetest thing ever," I tell her. "But also a little scary. I'm not ready for the whole duchess thing yet, so let's hope there are many years before we need to think about that."

Merry high-fives me and scoots off her stool.

"All right, I have to get busy," she says coolly. "Outta my kitchen!"

I snort-laugh and run away as she launches a playful swat in my direction.

With Merry happily busy in the kitchen, I decide to check on the bedrooms while Zach plants a quick kiss on my cheek as I leave. I head down the hall and up the large jack-and-jill staircase that leads to the second-floor bedrooms.

A team of maids from a local business called Clean Queens is working up here, and I smile at Maggie, their team lead, as she runs a vacuum on the carpet in the hall. They're all wearing hot pink t-shirts with the Clean Queens logo on them with black leggings, looking more adorable than I ever have while housecleaning.

"We're done with all the bedrooms up here," she tells me. "I have everyone working in the common rooms now."

I breathe a sigh of relief. Maggie and her team are the best.

"Thank you so much. I'll just grab a few things from my office and be out of their way."

Maggie nods and gets back to business as I duck into my office. There's another maid in here, dusting, and I grin at her as I grab a bunch of gift bags off my desk.

"Just here to pick these up," I explain. "I'll get out of your way."

She nods. "No problem."

I sweep back out into the hall and decide to start with the bedroom at the end. When Zach originally bought this estate years before he met me, the rooms were all named so the staff could keep track of them. Being British, Zach loved that feature, and he decided to keep up with it, so each door has a brass plaque with the room name on it. I step into the Irving bedroom, where my brother Max will be staying, and look through the gift bags in my hand until I find his.

I set all the gift bags down on the bed for a moment, then place his on the nightstand. I carefully move the tissue paper aside to make sure everything is there. His favorite snacks, a little bottle of hand sanitizer, a few chamomile tea bags, a little bottle of lavender pillow mist and, of course, red licorice. I also threw in a small bottle of ibuprofen since he's recovering from what he calls a "minor injury." He promised to fill me in when he gets here tonight, but I thought a painkiller might be a good idea.

I arrange the gift tag on the bag so that it's facing out and he'll see that it's printed with the schedule of events for the weekend. Then, I grab the other bags off the bed and head to the next room to repeat the process. Not all bags are the same, so I'm extra careful to put the right bags in the right rooms. There's a handful of peanut butter cups in Sam and Bella's bag. I made a point to add a personal touch to each of them.

Just as I'm finishing up, I hear a squeal downstairs. It's followed by a very recognizable laugh, and I rush out to the upstairs landing and head down with a huge grin as I prepare to hug Ashley and Rick. When I get to the bottom, I'm treated to the sight of Zach and Rick giving each other what I call a back-slapping dude hug. I run up behind Ashley, who is talking to Merry, and tickle her. She squeals and twirls around to hug me in return, and Merry throws herself in for good measure. Ashley pulls away first, heaving a happy sigh.

"Now we just need Scarlet, and my heart will be full," she says sweetly. "I've missed the four of us being together."

I nod in agreement. "It'll be good to have everyone in the same time zone for once."

Ashley grins as Rick pulls her against his side.

"This weekend is going to be so fun," she says. "Thanks for doing all this work."

Rick grins at me. "Is there anything we can do to help?"

I shake my head. "I think everything's under control, but that also scares me. Like…what if there's something I forgot?"

Merry nudges me. "Then we'll adapt, Duchess. Nothing has to be perfect. We'll all still love you, even if the napkins aren't folded perfectly."

I laugh under my breath. My friends know me so well. Since Zach will assume his father's title someday and be the Duke of Wendly, I will be a duchess. As an American who came from nothing, that's an intimidating thought, even if the future Duke of Wendly is a world-famous rockstar who doesn't care if I ever fold a napkin perfectly. It's nice to be reminded by those who love me that I never have to be perfect. I'm enough for them just as I am.

Merry breaks away from the group when the oven timer goes off, swiftly pulling a baking pan out and replacing it with another. Zach moves over to investigate the heavenly smells, and she playfully swats him away. I pull him close to me, and he comes willingly, growling in my ear and sending a familiar shiver down my spine.

"How's the book coming along, Ashley?" Merry asks as she spoons some kind of fluffy concoction into a pastry bag.

Ashley nods excitedly. "Better than I expected. I just got the manuscript back from my editor, and her notes are amazing. It's really exciting."

"Wow, that's so great," I say as I steal another hug. "I'm proud of you."

She beams with pride as Rick pulls her hand up and grazes a kiss across her knuckles.

"Tell them everything," he says with a proud smile.

The room quiets as we wait for her to share more.

"My editor thinks I should start looking for an agent," Ashley tells us with a bashful smile. "She thinks a publisher would be interested in it."

Merry runs around the kitchen island and presents Ashley with a freshly baked cookie on a napkin.

"You get a cookie just for being extra awesome."

I suppress a laugh at the crestfallen look on Zach's face when Ashley gets a cookie, and he doesn't. He tries to talk tough, but he's a sugar junkie. He'll never turn down a cookie. Or biscuits, as he calls them. I'll have to figure out a way to snag one for him later.

The day passes in the most wonderful blur of catch-up conversations long overdue. It makes me realize how proud I am of the home Zach and I have built here, and how wonderful it is to fill it with friends and family. It's nearing late afternoon now, and this has been one of the best days of my life.

We've been in the kitchen all day, most of us sitting around the island so we can keep Merry company. She's even let a few of us help a bit. I can't think of a better person to christen our new kitchen than Merry. It's been just as fun watching her work her magic as it has been visiting with everyone.

The doorbell rings, and I pull away from Zach to go answer it. I've hired Maggie and one of her team to stay on all weekend as a combination of butler and concierge for our guests. By the time everyone gets here, we'll have twelve people on the estate. I'm catering most of the meals because I can't cook, plus I hate it anyway. Hiring a caterer leaves me free to fuss over our guests.

Maggie's team will be on hand to help people settle in and then assist with clean-up and tidying rooms. I wouldn't have thought of it at all, but Zach threw a party or two in this house before we were a couple, and I'm so grateful he suggested it. They've already been lifesavers, but they're not really on duty for all that until this evening, and I don't want to be greedy and expect her to be on door duty right now.

I swing open the front door and welcome Sam and his wife, Bella. They're the last guests to arrive before we have a car service pick up Scarlet, Andrew, and Max late tonight. Sam and Bella roll their bags into our large foyer as Zach joins me, and hugs are exchanged all around. Zach grabs Sam and begins dragging him to the kitchen as Maggie comes galloping down the stairs. I gesture for Bella to follow the guys and turn towards Maggie.

"What room are they in?" she asks as she grabs their bags.

"I know you're busy up there," I tell her. "I can take this."

She laughs softly. "Zach warned me you'd do this. I've got it, Marina."

"Ugh, that man knows me so well. Thank you, Maggie…they're in the Crane room. I'll leave you to it."

I walk back to the kitchen and join the whole gang. The conversation has shifted to Jimmy and his longtime girlfriend, Beth.

"What does it matter if they're happy?" Rick tells Zach. "Marriage isn't for everyone. Maybe it's not for them."

I tilt my head and give my husband a knowing look, and he lets out a gravelly chuckle. He throws his hands up in surrender.

"I'm sorry, love, you caught me," he says. "I just want everyone I love to be as happy as I am."

I step into his arms and plant a sweet kiss on the corner of his mouth. Zach has long wondered why Jimmy has never proposed to his girlfriend, and they've been a couple for years and years. But Rick is

16

right. Marriage isn't for everyone, and they seem very happy together.

"Beth is a very successful leader at her company," I remind Zach. "I'm sure she's just fine with how things are."

Ashley nods. "She can still barely take her eyes off Jimmy whenever I see them together. I think they're so cute."

"Okay, okay, I'll shut up," Zach concedes with a chuckle.

"Zach, why don't you show Sam and Bella the Crane room while I take Rick and Ashley to the guest house?"

Zach wraps me in his arms for a quick hug and then motions for Sam and Bella to follow him upstairs.

I turn to my friends.

"I'm so sorry...I should have taken you back there when you arrived. I have you two in one of the guest houses on the back of the property, if that's okay," I explain. "The house will be a bit more chaotic and a little noisy."

Ashley grins. "I was planning on doing a little writing while I'm here, so that sounds perfect."

I nod. "Well, grab your bags and I'll take you out there."

Merry grabs the timer off the counter and chases after us.

"I'm coming too," she says. "I heard how great it looked when Scarlet decorated. I want to see it in person."

We head outside through the grand French doors. There's a wide path leading to one side of the pool. Once we pass the cascading water feature, a rock sculpture that flows into the deep end of the pool, we get to the garden and outdoor cooking spaces. Only then do we finally get a full glimpse of the two well-appointed guest houses at the back of the property. I hand Ashley a key and lead our group to the house on the right.

"You guys are in the Mermaid cottage," I explain as Ashley uses the key to open the door.

"What's the other cottage called?" Merry asks.

I grin before answering, "Rockstar. Scarlet and Andrew will be in that one."

I'm rewarded with a soft laugh from Merry.

"I love the names," she says as we step inside.

The small living area is decorated in hues of cream and lavender. There's a cozy loveseat facing a set of French doors overlooking the pool and garden. I step over to one side and call attention to the little drapery pull tucked to the side.

"There's a privacy curtain here in case you'd like to block the view into the cottage. I hate putting curtains on French doors, so Scarlet set this up and tucked it back here where it's hard to notice."

Ashley grins. "Our friend, the decor genius."

I step over to the tiny kitchen and point out the microwave, electric teapot, coffee maker, and other amenities. Then, we head back to the bedroom and bathroom. Ashley gasps as she sees the bathroom, all decorated in mermaid tones of lavender and deep purple. She shakes her head in wonder as she looks around, then she steps forward to get a better look at the framed print above the bathtub.

"Of course she did this," Ashley says with a grin, pointing to the framed lyrics of The Wellerman. "I love the personal touches she puts into projects."

I laugh softly. "She wanted to frame the mermaid tail and put it in there, but as soon as she mentioned framing it, I wanted it for my office at The Mermaid Foundation."

Merry nods. "That definitely seems a better fit for the thing that literally brought you and Zach together and started the foundation. Great idea."

We all step into the bedroom, and everyone is suitably impressed that Scarlet was able to fit a king-size bed in this space and still make it feel open. These two cottages aren't huge, but I wanted them to feel spacious and comfortable. She did a fantastic job on them. The walls are painted a light lavender that almost takes on a silvery appearance, and the lush, cream-colored bedding is accented with lavender throw pillows.

"We'll definitely be comfortable," Ashley tells me with a grin. "This is so beautiful, Marina."

"I'm pretty happy with the job Scarlet did on the cottages," I say with a nod. "Before we turned them into guest houses, Zach had one set up as a kind of storage facility for all his instruments, and the other was just empty. This is much better for when we have friends coming to stay."

Rick grins at me. "I'm so glad you sang in a traffic jam and got him out of the bus that day, Marina," he says sweetly. "You're definitely the best thing that's ever happened to that man."

My heart skips a few beats as happy memories flicker through my mind. I feel an enormous amount of gratitude for my life today, and I'm so thankful I was brave and took a chance on us. Especially since I only wanted to run away in the beginning.

"Well, he's stuck with me forever now."

The kitchen timer in Merry's hand begins to chime, and she holds it up and starts for the door.

"I'll go with you, Mer," I say as I follow. "You guys can unpack and relax. We'll see you at the house when you're ready."

"Thanks, girl," Ashley's voice trails after us as Merry and I head out the front door.

She silences the timer as we start up the path to the house. I'm not sure, but I feel like she's in a bit of a funk since we toured the guest house. The smell of maple wafts out from the house and I give her a nudge.

"I don't know what you're baking first, but it smells amazing."

Merry grins over at me. "The maple creme sandwich cookies."

"Mmm." I can already taste them. Those things are a favorite of mine.

"What do I have to do to get an early taste?"

Merry points back at the guest houses with a sarcastic grin as we step into the house together.

"Keep one of those ready for me? At the rate I'm going, I'll be the old spinster friend you have to make room for."

I hear voices and laughter coming from upstairs, so I know everyone else is out of earshot. I follow Merry to the kitchen and watch her pull out a baking pan and replace it with the next. Then I reach over and put my hands on her shoulders.

"First of all, I always have room for you," I say gently. "That will never change. And I know you love to joke, but I have faith that there's a good man out there somewhere with a Merry-shaped space in his heart that only you can fill."

Merry laughs softly and pulls me in for a hug before stepping away to fiddle with more ingredients. I get the hint, so I don't press the issue, but there's a little tendril of worry winding its way into my heart. When she does talk about her dating life, it's almost as if her usual spark leaves her eyes. Like, there's not much hope left...and to have our unicorn lose hope is not something I'm willing to let happen. Trouble is, I'm not sure what the plan should be.

Chapter 2

Zach

I pad downstairs after showing Sam and Bella to the Crane bedroom, unable to get the smile off my face. This is our first big party as a married couple in this house, and Marina is pulling out all the stops. Spoiler alert: she's killing it, and if I weren't madly in love with her already, I'd fall in love with her all over again. She's been incredible this week, but I worry about her being able to relax enough to actually enjoy this weekend with our friends. Good thing I'm excellent at keeping watch as a loving husband.

I creep into the kitchen in hopes that the girls are still at the guest house with Rick, and I can sneak one of Merry's incredible biscuits. It smells like she's been baking the maple ones with the creme filling that I adore. As soon as I get there, however, I can see my beautiful red-haired bride walking back toward the house with Merry. My eyes dart nervously between the biscuits lying on the baking sheet and the ladies' distance from the door. I briefly contemplate making a ninja move that would rival Tom Cruise in one of those Mission Impossible movies, but decide against it. I'd never make it in time, and Marina would know. I can't hide anything from her.

I duck back into the hallway and head to the library instead. I was talking to Rick about a book I just read, and I want to grab it for him. Plus, I have no desire to be seen unsupervised near Merry's baking. Why bring suspicion upon myself…especially when it'll result in tighter security measures. I may have a better opportunity later and want to keep my options open.

Book in hand, I head back to the kitchen and find Merry back to baking and Marina with a subtle little frown on her face. I set the book on the island and pull her against my side, planting a kiss on top of her beautiful head.

"Everything all right, my love?" I murmur against the softness of her hair.

Marina wraps an arm around my waist and nods, but I can feel that everything is definitely not all right. With Merry busy mixing ingredients, I give Marina a little squeeze, and she makes eye contact with me. The look on her face tells me enough. Talk later. I nod discreetly and turn my attention to our guest.

"Merry, you've made the house smell better than it ever has."

She gives me a smile and wiggles her eyebrows.

"And I'm just getting started."

I laugh in response as Marina nudges me and shows me her phone. Olivia, or Livvie, as we've nicknamed her, is messaging again, and she wants to know if we can do a quick video chat right now instead of later tonight. This kid is dear to us both, and the answer is unequivocally yes. Always.

"Merry, if anyone comes looking for us, we'll be in my study making a quick video call to Olivia," I tell her. Marina's already on her way. "We won't be but a few minutes."

Merry smiles and waves us off, and I follow Marina. Once we're inside the study, I push the door closed as Marina begins pacing. She looks up at me with a worried expression.

"Do you think she's okay? What do you think she wants to talk to us about?"

My darling Siren. Such a worrywart sometimes. I take her hand and tug on it until she steps into my arms.

"She's probably too excited about the talent show to wait until tonight, love. That's all."

Marina nods and chews on her lower lip. It's a nervous trait of hers that pulls on my heartstrings like no other. I quickly kiss the top of her head and take her hand, leading her over to my desk. I sit in the chair and pull her into my lap, then spin us a few times just to make her laugh. Her lilting voice calms me as she lets out a soft laugh. Mission accomplished.

I pull us up to the desk so she can work the keyboard and open a video call to Olivia. We could do this on our phones, but it's nice to be able to see her on the big monitor in here. It barely rings, and sweet Livvie's face fills the screen. She smiles at us excitedly.

"Hello, Livvie," Marina says sweetly. "Is everything all right?"

Livvie nods rapidly.

"Yes, I'm sorry if I'm bothering you."

I shake my head. "You are never bothering us. Are you just so excited about the talent show?"

Another nod. "I feel like I have a thousand feelings right now."

Marina grins at her. "Want to share some of them with us?"

Livvie positively beams, then nods. Identifying her feelings is something she's been working on with her therapist. We've been working together with her foster mum by asking questions like this and giving her space to use these skills.

"Definitely excited," she says brightly. "I've always wanted to do a talent show."

Marina nods enthusiastically. "That's so great. What else are you feeling?"

23

Livvie rolls her eyes up to the ceiling, and her tongue comes out of her mouth as she thinks. It's the cutest thing. She squints those deep brown eyes so hard. She's digging deep, looking for the words to identify her feelings.

"Happy, too," she says. "This girl Emily was helping Miss Lucien with the sign-ups and was really nice to me."

"Yeah?" I chime in. "What did she say?"

"She got all excited when I said I would be singing, and she said she's singing too," Livvie tells us. "I told her I wasn't sure what I was gonna sing yet, and she said she's singing Let It Go from Frozen. I promised not to copy her song, and she said I was really nice."

Marina puts her hand on my leg and squeezes, stealing a glance at me. There's such pride shining in her eyes, and I know it's because Livvie is such a sweet kid.

"That's very sweet of you, Livvie," Marina says. "You might be making a friend in Emily. Would that be okay?"

Livvie nods. "Yeah, she's cool. I like her a lot."

"Any other feelings you want to share, love?" I ask her.

Livvie thinks about it for a moment. "Scared, probably."

Marina leans forward a little. "That's okay, sweetheart. That's totally normal. Do you want to talk about it?"

More thinking is going on. "Okay."

We wait patiently for Livvie to find the words. This is the hardest part for me, because I'm just naturally inclined to keep conversations going. Being in Livvie's life is teaching me how to deal with kids and all the emotions they bring.

"I guess it's just scary to think about what if the kids don't like me? Like…what if I sing and they think it's stupid?"

"Yeah, that is scary," Marina says. "Lots of people would feel the same way. I was super scared the first time I got up on a stage."

Livvie nods. "Miranda said it was okay, too, but I still wanted to talk about it some more."

"Of course you did, love," I tell her gently. "We're so proud of you for talking about your feelings. It's a brave thing."

Livvie looks at us skeptically. "Easy for everyone else. I get angry and confused."

"Hey, hey, now," Marina says gently. "Everyone gets angry and confused once in a while. You just might not see them when it happens. It's a totally normal thing."

Livvie gets distracted by something on the other side of the camera, and she looks like she's caught with her hand in the biscuit jar. Er… cookie jar. She smiles feebly, then her foster mum sits on the couch beside her and waves at us.

"I'm so sorry, guys, I told her she needed to wait until your video chat tonight."

I laugh and shake my head. "It's no problem, Miranda, we promise."

Marina nods. "It really is okay. We're so excited for her, and she's never bothering us."

Miranda ruffles Livvie's hair and smacks a kiss on top of her head. "Okay, she has homework in five minutes. Don't let her forget."

We all laugh as Livvie makes a sour face, and Miranda bids us goodbye. Livvie looks at the camera again.

"I really am sorry that I took you away from your party."

"Livvie, it's okay, baby girl," Marina tells her. "You're excited and feeling all kinds of feelings. I love that you wanted to talk to us so soon. We wanted to talk to you, too."

Livvie heaves a great sigh of relief, which is adorable. She pushes her long, dark hair off her shoulder and smiles.

"Should we still keep our regular video date tonight before bed?" I ask her.

She nods excitedly. "Yes, please. I'll probably have like a thousand more feelings by then."

Marina and I burst into laughter.

"Oh, sweetie, you're the best," Marina says with a sigh. "We'll be waiting. Make sure you get all that homework done, smart girl. You got this."

Livvie makes a face and then grins at us mischievously.

"Thanks again, you guys."

"Go Team Livvie!" I cheer as she waves and giggles, then disconnects.

I immediately pull Marina against me, reveling in the feel of her body relaxing into mine.

"See, my darling? Everything was all right."

I feel her heave a great sigh and let it out, and I press a kiss to the side of her head.

"I wish we could have brought her here," Marina sighs. "I miss her."

There are strict rules with children who are in the foster system, as Marina well knows since she grew up that way. They can't travel anywhere without special permission.

I rub my hand up Marina's back to soothe her, and she shivers ever so slightly.

"She'll be all right," I say soothingly. "Miranda's a wonderful foster mum."

Marina sits up with a soft smile on her lovely face. "She sure is. She works miracles with any kid that comes to her."

I nod. "Right. So let's not worry. Let's just be proud and happy for Livvie."

I'm rewarded with a bright smile now.

"You're right," she says, slipping from my lap before I can protest. "Let's go, baby. We've got people to take care of this weekend."

I push myself out of my chair and follow my beautiful wife to the door. Before she can open it, I reach over quickly and pull her against me. I hold her with one arm and raise my pinky finger in front of her.

"Team Livvie?" I ask, prompting a beautiful laugh.

She hooks her pinky finger around mine.

"Team Livvie."

Marina gasps. "I almost forgot to tell you. Merry made another spinster joke about herself, and it just kills me. I hate this for her."

I take Marina's hands in mine and give them a reassuring squeeze.

"There's not much you can do to help if she says no interference. Just keep listening and supporting."

Marina opens the door to the study, and we step out into the hall. The voices of our friends float out from the kitchen. They must have all joined Merry. Marina halts just outside the study and gives me a hopeful look.

"Is it really interfering if she's already met the guy, though? Hillary's brother is single, and he's so sweet."

I take a step back and give her what she calls "the stink eye".

"I really got the feeling Merry is serious about the interfering. She might get upset if you don't respect her wishes, baby."

Marina lets out a frustrated sigh.

"I know, I just...I really want to help. I hate that she seems so defeated."

"Merry's made of tough stuff, Siren," I remind her. "I think she'll be all right. Let's give her the space to do what's best for her."

Marina's response is a smile brighter than the sun.

"Look at you giving all of us ladies the space we need. That class on foster kids really got to you, didn't it?"

I laugh lowly and lace our fingers together.

"It's hard work, but I have to make sure I'm keeping up with you, my darling."

We head off to the kitchen together to join our friends.

***

"Wait a minute..." Ashley says in an incredulous tone. "Not only did he hate all sweets, but he hated Italian food as well?"

27

Merry nods and rolls her eyes.

"I can't make this stuff up," she says as she pipes cream filling into her sandwich cookies. "Like…my profile literally said I am a baker and I'm an Italian working at an Italian restaurant that's been in my family for generations. Why would he even send me a message in the first place?"

Ashley shakes her head in disbelief. "But you didn't actually go out with that one?"

Merry laughs.

"No, thankfully. I told him thanks, but no thanks."

I pull out an empty counter stool for Marina and nudge her until she sits.

Relax, woman.

"What app is it?" I ask nonchalantly.

Partly because I want to know, but mostly because I know Marina wants to know and feels like she can't ask.

Merry shakes her head. "I deleted my profile. I'm taking a break from all of that. It's exhausting. The Spinster DeLuca is tired."

I guess I have a worried look on my face because Merry runs over and pats me on the shoulder before continuing her work.

"I'm just taking a break, Zach. It's okay. I'm not throwing in the towel. I'm just tired of kissing a lot of toads."

I was hoping this conversation would make Marina feel a little better about not trying to help, but I think I've just made it worse. Mercifully, the doorbell rings and distracts us all. Marina moves in her seat, but I put my hands firmly on her shoulders and lower my lips to her ear.

"You stay and enjoy yourself," I murmur, softly kissing the shell of her ear. "I'll get it, my darling."

I'm rewarded with a kiss on my cheek, and I turn away from our friends and head to the door. Little tingles dance across my skin where Marina's soft lips were. Heaven.

I open the door and find Jimmy and Beth on the porch in a bit of a tryst. They're passionately kissing, and I'm torn between walking away and leaving the door open so they can let themselves in…or tossing a bucket of water on them. Thankfully, Beth realizes they have an audience and breaks away from her lesser half. I grin at them both.

"Well, well, well," I tease. "What a show that was."

Beth laughs and gives me a playful shove.

"And I was going to tell you the news first," she whispers as she steps into the foyer. "Maybe I won't."

"News? I'm all ears."

Jimmy rolls their suitcase in as Maggie descends the stairs with perfect timing and takes the bag. I smile at Maggie and point to my friends.

"Jimmy and Beth, not sure which room."

Maggie smiles. "I have a list, no worries."

I step closer to Beth and Jimmy as Maggie disappears up the stairs.

"What news?"

Beth looks at Jimmy for a moment. He grins and nods, then she turns to me and holds her left hand up for inspection. There appears to be a ten-pound diamond weighing down her finger.

"Good lord, it's happened!" I exclaim as I wrap Beth in a tight hug. "Many congratulations, love!"

Beth is positively giddy as she hugs me back, and I'm pretty sure I spy a little moisture in Jimmy's eyes. I release Beth and nearly jump on top of Jimmy as I hug him. It's just our way. My whole body vibrates as he chuckles and squeezes me tight. I slap him on the back and break away, beaming at both of them.

"Well, come into the kitchen and spread the news. This is amazing."

I can't contain my excitement, so I run ahead of them while wildly clapping my hands to get everyone's attention. Before the hugging starts, I hold my hands up to keep everyone in their places.

"Jimmy and Beth have something to say."

Jimmy rolls his eyes at me and laughs, and Beth is so excited she does a cute little dance in her spot as he wraps his arms around her. The whole group eyes them expectantly, and I suddenly wish I had my phone on me to capture this moment on video.

Beth takes a deep breath and holds her left hand up, wiggling her ring finger for extra emphasis, and the whole room goes absolutely insane. Screams. Squeals. Shrieks. It's all happening in our kitchen.

I stand back and watch our friends for a moment, waiting for Marina to get her hugs in, and then gently pulling her into my arms. She turns so her back is against my chest, and we stand together as we listen to Beth tell the story.

"I didn't want us to get married until I was ready to leave my job," she explains. "CFO isn't a job that gives a lot of free time, at least not at a large corporation like mine."

I wouldn't know, of course, but I can only imagine. From the outside, I've always thought they make their relationship work flawlessly. I've never known them to fight or even argue, and they make time for each other even with our band's tour schedule and her demanding job.

"I've made enough money for myself," Beth continues. "And I'm the youngest CFO in the history of Textech. I've made my mark. To be honest, it hasn't been fun for a while…and I was sitting in a meeting last week when I realized I don't want to do it anymore."

Jimmy pulls her hand up to his lips and kisses the back of it.

"She took a few days off to come and see me," he shares. "And she told me she was going to give her notice. I got up from the couch and went to the bedroom to get the ring I've been holding onto for five years…and I proposed right then and there."

The collective sigh coming from the women in the room is completely adorable. Beth laughs softly.

"Okay, I did give a one-year notice," she explains. "I owe them a lot. It's been a great job and I care a lot about my team. I'll help with the hiring process and the onboarding, and then I'm gone. Ready for another chapter."

"I'm so happy for you guys," Marina says with a little wobble in her voice. "Will it be a traditional wedding? What will you do after you leave your job? I have so many questions."

Beth laughs softly. "So do we! There's a lot to figure out, but we're working through what things look like when I leave Textech. But yes...very traditional wedding with all the Rebels as groomsmen, of course."

Jimmy steps over to my side with a disgustingly happy grin. I'm so chuffed for him and Beth. They deserve all the happiness in the world.

"Can I steal a moment with just the Rebels?" Jimmy asks in a near whisper.

I nod. "I'll grab Sam, you get Rick. Beers on the patio?"

Jimmy nods. "See you in a few."

I head to the fridge first and grab four bottles of my favorite local IPA. I pass behind Marina, who watches me curiously, and lean in close to whisper to her.

"Special Rebels toast, love...be right back."

She nods in understanding. I give Sam a quick head nod to follow me, and he leaves Bella to chat with the ladies while we head out the French doors to the patio. It's chilly, but rather nice after the excitement of the big announcement.

Jimmy and Rick each take a beer from me, and I hand the last one to Sam as we step take the steps down and walk nearer the garden. Finally Jimmy stops, and we all gather around to clink our bottles together.

"Congratulations, man. I'm so happy for you two," Rick says fondly.

"About time," Sam jokes, making us all snicker.

"Thanks, guys," Jimmy says quietly. "I'm a lucky man, but I know you three understand how this feels."

With Sam and me happily married and Rick heading down the aisle early next year, we certainly do, but I sense Jimmy has more to share. He tends to be fairly tight-lipped, so I decide to help him a bit.

"Out with it, lad."

Jimmy laughs. "You know me so well, dude."

Rick, Sam, and I wait for more.

"There's more to share," Jimmy says soberly. "Beth will take a year to leave her company, but we're allowing for eighteen months, really. She's a planner, my girl. She's comfortable with that."

Sam nods. "As someone who is married to a planner, I recommend you just go with it. But I know you know this."

"For sure. But...I wanted to talk to you guys about something."

The air turns heavy between us as Jimmy's expression grows more serious. He's nervous about something, which doesn't happen often.

"Hey, Jim," I say gently, clapping a hand on his shoulder and squeezing. "It's just us. Whatever it is, you know the drill. We support you. So spill it."

Jimmy nods, swallowing hard.

"When Beth leaves her job, we want to take a year off to travel. Maybe longer."

Ah. There it is. The real meaning of this moment settles in the air all around us. Our days of being The Royal Rebels are now numbered.

Rick nods soberly. "Well...we always knew this would happen eventually, right?"

We all nod, and I give Jimmy's shoulder another squeeze as I look him in the eye.

"We did. Absolutely. And it's okay, Jim."

He looks around at all of us. "Yeah?"

Sam nods. "Yeah. What did we always say? Brothers first, band second."

I grin and nod in agreement. Brothers. Because we've been more than friends since college. None of us could have known how successful The Royal Rebels would be, and we agreed to take it as far as we could until life pulled us in other directions. Before anyone knew who we were. When we were just four guys writing songs and playing wherever we could.

"Brothers first and always, mate," I say to the group. "Are we still in agreement that we'll do special projects together? The occasional reunion concert?"

Jimmy throws an arm around my shoulders.

"Try to stop me."

I notice a slow, sly grin spreading across Rick's face.

"What is it?"

"Jimmy, you think you really might push it to eighteen months?" he asks.

"Absolutely. Why?"

Rick looks at Sam with that same grin.

"How much would Bella kill us if we wanted to do one big final tour?"

Laughter peels out of Sam so hard he nearly falls over. I love this idea. It'll take planning and a lot of hard work, but our team can do it. Our fans will demand it.

"I think she might kill us if we say no. It's the first thing she'll think of when we tell her we're moving on."

"You guys are really okay with this?" Jimmy asks. "I thought I might be letting you down."

Sam shakes his head. "I can't imagine a thing any of you could do to let me down. Maybe the fact that we're not really going to stop working together helps. It's just going to look different when you get married, that's all."

Jimmy snorts. "A lot different."

Rick shrugs. "Zach and I will keep writing. I hope we all keep playing separately, but we'll have reunion gigs we can do and...well, we won't be done with each other. Ever. I'm okay with this."

I nod. "Me too. Very okay."

Jimmy shakes his head. "Wow. Another big tour. Not gonna lie… sounds like a great way to go out. It's gonna be fun."

Sam steps into the middle of our small circle and puts his arms out. "All right then, come on…big Rebel hug."

We all close the distance and wrap our arms around each other, then step back. Rick holds up his beer.

"Cheers to the big tour, guys."

We all clank our bottles again, simultaneously giving cheers, and then the conversation turns to Jimmy's wedding. They want to do it in the Maldives, which sounds beautiful, but that's a long flight. My back hurts just thinking about it. It'll be worth it to be there for Jimmy and Beth, though. Not to mention having Marina all to myself in one of those luxury over-water bungalows. I can't imagine anything better.

After a few more minutes, we start wandering our way back to the house. I feel such gratitude tonight, more so because of Jimmy and Beth's announcement and being surrounded by our loved ones. Our lives are changing, that's just the way things work. If it wasn't Jimmy's wedding leading to our retirement, my eventual dukedom would have done it. The things that really, truly matter aren't going away. They're changing. And for that, I'm so very grateful.

Chapter 3

Marina

I feel a light tap on the back of my arm and turn to find Maggie with an apologetic smile on her face. I motion for her to follow me over near the pantry, away from the friendly banter of my friends.

"The caterers are here, and they're setting up for cocktail hour in the library as you requested."

I have one of those moments when I wonder how on earth this is my life. *The caterers have arrived, and they're setting up cocktails in the library.* Sounds like something from a novel, not my actual life.

"Great, thanks so much, Maggie," I reply, giving her a grateful squeeze on her arm. "I already don't know what I'd do without you."

Maggie grins. "They said to tell you they'll be ready at the scheduled time and asked if the kitchen will be ready for them while you're having cocktails."

I nod. "We'll be out of here for sure."

Maggie nods and excuses herself to chat with the caterers. I step back to the kitchen island where everyone is gathered. Merry is putting her famous maple creme cookies into storage containers, and I marvel at how many there are. I say another silent prayer that Nonno finally gives in and lets her open the bakery attached to his restaurant. Her talents are being wasted otherwise.

"I'm just putting these up for tomorrow," she says, as if reading my mind. "I'll have this all cleaned up in ten. I'll prep the mini pies in the morning. Didn't you say you had a second fridge where I could put things?"

"Yep. There's a fridge in the outdoor kitchen on the deck."

Merry snorts. "Dude, remember when you were freaked out that you'd get fired by the Evil Queen and wouldn't make rent on your apartment in that sketchy neighborhood? Now you have a hot husband and an outdoor kitchen."

I laugh hysterically. "Wow, I haven't thought about her in a thousand years."

"Good riddance," Merry says.

I nod. "Good riddance. I'm happy with my hot husband. The outdoor kitchen is just a bonus."

Zach sneaks up behind me and growls in my ear, sending little shivers down my spine. Delicious shivers. Merry grins at me and zooms away. Her arms are loaded with containers of cookies, but Ashley follows and opens the French doors for her.

I turn in Zach's arms and smile up at him.

"What were you guys talking about out there so seriously?"

Zach leans in and rubs our noses together.

"Weddings and the future," he murmurs. "I'll tell you everything tonight, Siren."

I steal a quick kiss from him, then take a deep breath. This is our first big party on the estate, and I've done so much planning for it. I'm excited that it's finally here, and I'm also excited to have my closest friends under our roof this weekend. It's going to be a great time.

"So what are we doing this weekend?" Rick asks as he and Sam step closer. "Bobbing for apples? Do we get to go trick-or-treating?"

I shake my head at Rick. "I hope you brought a great costume, though, because we are definitely dressing up on Halloween night."

"Is there a prize for the best one? Ashley and I are contenders for sure."

I raise my eyebrows. "Oh? What are you dressing as?"

"Nope," Rick replies. He points at Ashley, who's chatting with Beth. "I'm sworn to secrecy by that beautiful blonde over there."

Zach laughs. "Your better half."

Rick grins. "No doubt."

"Our neighbor has invited us to a hockey game tomorrow night," Zach adds. "He gave me six tickets, so I thought the guys could go together."

Rick frowns. "How did your neighbor end up with six tickets to a hockey game that he can't use? I assume it's the local team?"

Zach gives a quick nod. "The Hudson Valley area's finest. My neighbor owns the AHL team."

Rick's laugh booms through the kitchen. "I should have guessed he owns the team if he's your neighbor."

"He's a good, solid guy. I don't know him well, but I like him. Want to guess what the team is called?"

Sam looks thoughtful for a moment, then replies, "The Ichabod Cranes?"

I laugh and shake my head. "Close. The Horsemen."

"Okay, that's just cool. I love it. And a hockey game sounds like fun. I'm in," Rick replies.

"Me too," Sam says. "I love hockey."

"I'm a little jealous," I tell them. "But I have fun things planned for the ladies, so you guys enjoy yourselves."

"And what are you ladies doing?" Sam asks me.

"We're heading into town and getting crafty," I tell him. "Then drinks, shopping, you name it. We'll meet you guys back here for dinner."

Sam smirks. "I am definitely not crafty. Sounds terrible. Hockey's way better."

I snort and give him a light shove. "Whatever, Sam. Your loss."

He tilts his head and gives me an evil grin. "Bella's not super crafty either. You may be sorry."

I raise my chin. "Can't scare me. We're going to have a great time."

"Don't say I didn't warn you, Marina," Sam says with a snicker.

I just roll my eyes at him and grin. Bella's wonderful. Even if she's not crafty, I know she'll make the best of it, and she'll have fun with us.

I glance at the clock in the kitchen and see that it's time for cocktails, but I just want to be sure they're ready for us. I step back from the group and make my way to the hall that leads to the library, but I don't have to go far.

The catering staff are all waiting in the hall with Maggie.

Maggie gives me a thumbs up, and I mouth the words *thank you* and duck back into the kitchen. I clap my hands together to get everyone's attention.

"All right, friends, I am officially beginning our Halloween fun by inviting you to join me for cocktails. This way, please."

I love the expectant smiles on their faces as my friends follow me into the hall. The catering staff have disappeared, and I know they've gone to the kitchen through the great room to keep out of our way.

It's pretty dark outside now, so the room is going to look incredible. Zach steps up to the closed doors with me. He smiles widely at our guests.

"Happy Halloween weekend, friends!" he exclaims as we throw the doors open to reveal a fully-haunted library.

Everyone gasps, and I have to seriously fight the urge to squeal in excitement. We worked so hard on these decorations, and they look incredible. Our friends file inside slowly, looking all around at what we've done as Zach and I watch excitedly.

Ghosts made of white chiffon hang from the high, elaborately detailed ceilings. Zach and I worked for two days to strategically place black lights behind the ghosts so they'd have an eerie glow in the darkened space. Spiderwebs are everywhere, and I spent last weekend making fake, scary-looking books to place in random spots. Some have monster hands coming out of them. Some are dripping with green ooze. Some even have fangs. They also glow in the dark under the lights. We used fishing line to suspend remote-controlled, battery-operated candles from the ceiling, which gives the illusion that they're floating in mid-air.

To complete our haunted library, I asked the caterers to create Halloween-inspired cocktails for this evening. The mobile bar they moved in is elaborately decorated with black ivy and purple skulls. A cauldron sits in the center with dry ice bubbling and churning, fog spilling over the edge.

Even when it's not decorated for Halloween, this room is extremely large and very beautiful. In addition to the walls lined with bookcases, there are lateral bookcases in the middle of the room. Over by a huge picture window, there are four sofas, all facing inward, arranged around a square coffee table. Cozy, overstuffed chairs are also dotted throughout the room.

Merry rushes past me with an excited grin. I know what she's looking for. I gave her the inside scoop on what to expect for the weekend, and I know she's in search of the charcuterie skeleton that the catering team placed on the coffee table in the sitting area. I hear her squeal of delight, but I'm distracted by Ashley's touch on my elbow.

"This is incredible, my friend," she says in a reverent tone. "You've decorated this so well, you may make Scarlet jealous when she sees it."

I shake my head as we walk together towards the bar.

"Who do you think most of the ideas came from? We were texting like mad for days," I confess. "I knew she didn't have time to come and do it, but I also knew she'd have some great ideas. She did not disappoint. I hope she loves it."

"Oh, she will!"

We wait for Jimmy and Beth to step away from the bar with their drinks, then Ashley smiles at the bartender.

"Can I have a margarita, please?" she asks.

"Of course, madam," he replies in a sort of cartoony, ghoulish voice.

The catering company offered to have their staff dressed in costume, but I kept flashing back to my days of being trapped in that horrible mermaid tail. Even though it worked out well for me, I still didn't want anyone to have to deal with a costume that might be a real pain. Instead, I opted for simple black-and-white uniforms. The manager I worked with to set up the party suggested the staff members throw their personalities into being spooky while serving cocktails and dinner, and I was entirely on board with that.

"That sounds good, can you make that two?" I smile at him, but I feel it fade away when he turns that eerie look on me. He's so good at this.

He grins at me, and it's so delightfully creepy. He mixes two margaritas while Ashley looks around in awe, pointing out the various decorations and giving me endless praise for how it all came together. Finally, our drinks are handed over, and I am once again impressed at the amazing job these caterers are doing.

Our drinks are served in large margarita glasses that feature a light in the base, making them glow eerily. It's fabulous.

"These are so amazing," I tell the bartender with a huge grin. "Well done."

He gives me another creepy grin, and Ashley and I laugh as we walk away and step deeper into the room.

"This room is gorgeous," Ashley says breathlessly. "If this were my home, I'd live in here."

I laugh softly as we look around at the dark-stained, antique wood bookshelves lining all the walls. The lateral bookcases in the center of the room are stained in the same dark color, bringing them all together. The library was gorgeous already, but when Zach and I got married, I had Scarlet come over to suggest updates. So there's an accent wall covered in sumptuous floral wallpaper with gold accents. She also helped me find suitable furniture and decor that matched the style of the permanent fixtures. In the rest of the rooms, I felt very comfortable just going with my natural taste. This space is extraordinary, though, and I knew Scarlet would give the best advice on how to showcase it like the treasure it is.

"I used to think Zach was crazy for buying a whole estate like this until I visited the first time," I confess. "A home like this definitely appealed to him because he grew up in a noble British family, but I love the fact that this beautiful old home is still here. And it's ours. The history of it is preserved. Which is saying something because in America, we do love to tear things down and rebuild them."

Ashley chuckles. "Remember that piece of a Roman wall we just stumbled upon in London?" Ashley says as we sit together on one of the couches. "I still can't believe they just built a huge, modern office building around it because they didn't want to knock it down. That's so cool."

I nod. "I love that they do that. Every time Zach and I go visit his family, I insist we spend a day or two in London so I can explore it more."

"I would too."

We each take a sip of our margaritas, and I nearly choke at the smirk on her face. Ashley's known for being a little heavy-handed with the tequila whenever we have an emergency conclave of the four girlfriends. Granted, if there's a conclave, it's usually because one of us is having a crisis, but she loves to play bartender.

"Not enough tequila for you, dragon lady?" I joke.

Ashley laughs. "No, it's fine. Stop teasing. And I haven't been the dragon lady in a long time, girl."

I nod and take another sip. That's true enough. Rick tamed the dragon lady a long time ago. Now they're madly in love with each other and will walk down the aisle in the spring. I can't wait to be there for her and watch her on her special day.

"You have outdone yourself, my friend," Bella croons as she drops herself onto the sofa next to me. "This is freaking awesome."

I wiggle in my seat excitedly. "I'm so glad you guys like it. I wanted to kick the weekend off with a great start."

Bella chuffs. "You've set the bar incredibly high. I can't wait to see what's next. I mean…look at this!"

She sweeps her hand over the coffee table at the charcuterie skeleton. The caterers used a great-looking plastic skeleton, laid it on a large serving board, and covered it in meat, cheese, fruit, and veggies. It looks fun without being gruesome. There's a stack of plates on the table as well, and I reach over to grab a few. I pass one to Ashley, one to Bella, and keep one for myself.

"If you heard that squeal earlier, it was Merry," I tell them as I dish up a little plate for myself. "She knew about the skeleton and was so excited to see it."

I look around for her, but can't seem to find her.

"I can't blame her," Ashley says as she plucks a few pepperoni from the skeleton's rib cage. "I've never seen a dead guy look so delicious."

Bella laughs as she fills her plate with cheese cubes of various flavors. I go for the bacon I specifically requested because, well, I'm me. My love for bacon is a thing I don't hide.

"How's the wedding planning going, Ash?" Bella asks as she settles into the cushions. "Rick says the ceremony will be at the Palace of Fine Arts? That's going to be gorgeous."

Ashley pops a cheese cube into her mouth and nods with a blissfully happy smile. She chews, swallows, and lets out a sweet sigh.

"Let's be clear," she begins. "I would marry Rick at the courthouse tomorrow. Or in some tiny little church in the middle of nowhere. Or in Vegas-"

"We get it, girl," Bella says with an apologetic grin, holding a hand up. "Keep going."

Bella's a straight-to-the-point woman. It's why she's earned the nickname "Hella Bella" in the entertainment industry as the band's manager. Ashley laughs out loud and high-fives her.

"I love how you keep us all on track," Ashley says. "Anyway, a tiny little wedding was never in the cards with my dad. He has always wanted to send me off to married life in grand style, and so that's how it's going to be."

"I love him so much," I say with a shake of my head. "He's the sweetest."

Ashley grins. "When I was a little girl, playing with my dolls, I think he talked about my wedding more than I did."

The three of us break into laughter immediately. I can totally see him doing that. Ashley is his whole world, and it shows. He's a great father, and he's become a father figure to me, Merry, and Scarlet as well. We all call him Dad, or some version of it. Scarlet likes to call him Daddio. We all love him dearly. When he walks her down the aisle, there won't be a dry eye in all of San Francisco.

I look around for Merry again. Beth is chatting with Jimmy and Zach. Rick and Sam are pointing at the floating candles, trying to figure out how they work. The bartender and a server are chatting. I really don't see Merry anywhere. I excuse myself and head towards the door, looking into the little alcoves between bookcases to see if she's lost herself looking at all the books in here. Still no Merry.

I leave the library and walk out into the hall. I listen for a moment to see if I hear anyone upstairs, but I don't. I hear movement in the kitchen, but that would be the catering staff preparing for the dinner service. Then I hear Merry laugh…and it's coming from the kitchen.

I pause for a moment, thinking over the events of the evening and hoping there's been nothing to make her feel sad. Merry's sacred space is the kitchen. *Any* kitchen. It's why she loves to bake. The kitchen is where she makes sense of the world. I can't help feeling that I might be responsible somehow. She's been a little fragile lately, and with Jimmy and Beth's engagement announcement tonight, I realize it might all be too much for her. She's surrounded by couples in love.

Emotion clogs my throat as I realize I owe her a huge apology. I should have been more thoughtful as I planned tonight's activities. Maybe we could have played a game, breaking up the couples so that no one was paired with their significant other. My mind races with all the things I should have done.

"Siren?" Zach says softly as he steps out into the hall.

His arms, warm and solid, wrap around me.

"What's wrong, my darling?"

I sink against him and wrap my arms around his waist, inhaling his fresh, clean, beachy scent. It calms me like nothing else.

"Merry's in the kitchen with the caterers," I say quietly. "She usually cooks or bakes when she's upset."

Zach pulls away just enough to look into my eyes. Warm brown eyes watch me with concern.

"Why should she be upset?"

I shake my head. "I don't know. Maybe I should have-"

Zach gives my shoulders a squeeze.

"Baby, go talk to her before you tie yourself in a knot," he says softly. "Okay? It could be nothing."

I take a deep breath. I know he's right. It's just that my girlfriends mean the world to me. There's nothing I wouldn't do for Ashley, Scarlet, or Merry. I can't bear the idea that I caused her to be sad, even if it wasn't intentional. I nod slowly and step out of Zach's embrace.

"You're right," I tell him, which I know he loves to hear because it doesn't happen often. I give him a mock warning glare when he flashes me a delighted grin.

"Go check on her, love," Zach purrs. "And then come back to me."

This man. He gets my pulse pounding so easily. I give his arm a squeeze and head down the hall towards the kitchen. I slow my pace as I draw nearer, trying to hear whether anyone is consoling her. She was laughing, though, I'm sure of it. That can't be a bad sign.

"It's beautiful," a woman's voice says. "You've got some crazy skill."

Merry laughs again. "Thank you for letting me crash in your workspace. It was really kind of you."

"Hey, it was worth it just to watch you work," a man's voice says. "You sure you don't want a job?"

More laughter. It really does sound okay. I take a deep breath and head into the kitchen. I round the corner and find Merry standing at the end of the kitchen counter with a piping bag in her hand as four of the catering staff watch her. All heads turn to me when I walk in, and Merry's face lights up with a huge, beautiful smile.

"Hey, Marina, come see!"

I smile pensively and step over to her as the catering staff breaks up. Suddenly, they're busy with other tasks, and Merry holds her hands up to show a gorgeous layered cake with delicate flowers all over it. The base frosting is a very pale pink, and the flowers are all cream-colored. Pearl candies of varying sizes are dotted across the sides of the cake. My eyes fill with tears when I read the words *Congrats, Jimmy & Beth* that she's written in cream-colored icing.

"You don't have to give it to them if you don't want to," Merry says quickly. "But when we were all in here talking earlier, I thought it might be a nice touch."

I gulp down a hard swallow and nod, managing a wobbly smile. As long as I've known Merry, she's been such a selfless friend. She always thinks of others. This is so absolutely like her. I shake my head at the work of art in front of me.

"This is so gorgeous," I whisper, smiling at her.

She grins proudly. "You like it? I'm sure you planned dessert for later, so I can give it to them tomorrow sometime if—"

I push at her playfully. "No. This is so beautiful, Merry. Let's give it to them after dinner tonight."

"Yeah?"

I pull my friend into a hug. "Yeah."

Merry's arms wrap around me, and she gives me a good squeeze. "Can I ask you a question then?"

I pull away and nod. "Of course."

Merry watches me carefully, her brow furrowing a bit.

"Why are you crying, dude?"

I laugh self-consciously and wipe a tear from my cheek.

"I thought maybe I made you feel left out somehow," I confess, instantly noting her shocked expression. "And you came in here to get away from us, and instead I'm instantly reminded of your huge heart and infinite kindness."

Merry tilts her head at me. "You could never make me feel left out. Don't ever think that."

I nod. "Sorry. You're right."

"Open your mouth."

I don't bother hiding the shocked expression on my face. "What?"

She raises her eyebrows. "Do it."

I open my mouth, and Merry lifts the piping bag full of frosting, shooting some into my mouth. I pull back with a laugh.

"Dude…"

Merry laughs. "I'm sorry, but you were getting way too serious for a party. You needed a sugar fix."

I let the delectable frosting melt in my mouth and nod appreciatively. "That is some seriously good frosting."

Merry snorts. "You bet it is."

I snatch the bag from her hand and squirt another dollop into my mouth. Merry cackles and claps her hands together. One of the servers steps around us to retrieve something from the counter.

"Okay, this cake is done, and we need to get out of their way," Merry proclaims. She grabs my elbow and starts pulling me out of the kitchen. "Let's get back to the party."

"Gladly," I tell her. "Even though it's not quite a party yet."

Merry stops in her tracks for a moment, then she grins at me when she gets my meaning.

"Scarlet."

I nod. "Scarlet."

Merry grins. "And Andrew, let's not forget him."

"Or Max," I say. "Don't forget my baby brother."

Merry loops her arm through mine as we make our way back to the library.

"Right," she says. "So let's get back to the pre-party and have some cocktails."

My heart is positively overflowing as we enter the library together. Merry gives me another quick squeeze.

"This looks freaky good, my friend," she whispers in my ear. "I can't wait for Scarlet to see it."

I nod excitedly. "Me too."

"When is she due to arrive?"

I glance at my watch. "Late, but it couldn't be helped. I'm sure they'll all want to go straight to bed. We'll see them in the morning."

Merry grins at me. "Don't worry about that. She's so organized, she probably got to the airport in time to help the pilot with the pre-flight check."

I chuckle to myself as Merry runs off toward the skeleton charcuterie again. She's right, of course. I never have to worry about Scarlet. Zach's smoldering gaze locks with mine across the room, and my face blooms into a bright smile as I make my way across the library and into the arms of the man I love. This weekend is going to be epic, and I can't wait to spend it with the people I keep close in my heart.

II

Scarlet & Andrew

Chapter 4

Scarlet

I grumble in frustration for the umpteenth time this afternoon. Nothing is where it's supposed to be, and this is just my own personal nightmare. I hate being disorganized, but thanks to my busy work schedule, I've been living in chaos for weeks. I look at my open suitcase and give it a good glare, as if it's responsible for the fact that I can't find anything.

To be fair, we only just moved into this house a few months ago, and I had to hit the ground running. We hired movers, and then Andrew and I went right to work unpacking and decorating the common areas of the house. Then I went back to work, shooting my interior design TV show in various locations across the country. I'd pop back home most weekends, or Andrew would come and stay with me on location. We got things unpacked and decorated enough to hold our wedding here, but somewhere along the way, our bedroom was completely forgotten. And now I'm paying the price.

"Hey, beautiful," Andrew croons from the doorway, making me jolt.

His expression sours as he realizes how jumpy and stressed out I am, and he pushes off the door jamb with a singular purpose. Strong arms pull me against his muscular chest, and I let myself lean against him. His warm hands rub my back as he looks at me with concern.

"How can I help?" he murmurs sweetly.

I shake my head. "I can't find anything, and I hate it."

Andrew looks down at the suitcase on the bed.

"I see clothes, jammies, and our Halloween costumes," he says. "I even see undies. What are you missing?"

I know what's coming. My new husband is just not as fastidious about some things as I am. I purse my lips together to fight the stupid grin that threatens to betray me, holding up a pair of blue panties.

"For one thing, I can't find the bra that matches these."

A slow, sexy smile spreads across Andrew's face.

Hello, dimples.

He nods at the clock on the bedside table.

"Baby, we need to get going to the airport in fifteen minutes," he says gently. "I think you can survive a weekend without matching underwear."

Without making a big deal of it, he plucks the panties from my hand and neatly folds them. He's right, but I'm still annoyed at myself. Wordlessly, I begin folding what's left on the bed. He helps, and when we're done, he looks around the room.

"Do you need anything else?"

I take a deep breath and sigh heavily.

"I guess not. I think we're good to go."

The doorbell rings. That'll be my friend Rachel. She's taking us to the airport and staying in the house so our cat, Teeny, won't be alone. Andrew kisses me quickly, then turns me toward the bedroom door.

"You go let Rachel in, and I'll bring this along. Deal?"

I smile appreciatively. "I love you. Deal."

"I love you too," he says sweetly as I head out of the room.

I heave another sigh. This weekend is going to be great. All of us back together, most of us with our significant others in tow. I can't wait to just relax and hang out, even if I'm wearing mismatched undies the whole time.

***

An hour later, Andrew and I hastily wave goodbye to Rachel as she pulls away from the curb after dropping us off at the small airport where The Royal Rebels' private jet will take us to New York. Andrew grabs our suitcase, and I pull up the instructions Marina texted me as we make our way inside the terminal building. It's calm and quiet inside, at least when compared to a busy airport like San Francisco. I can definitely understand the appeal of traveling this way.

"Wow," Andrew mutters as he follows closely. "I feel fancy all of a sudden."

I laugh under my breath and nod as we approach a uniformed employee at the gate.

"Me too."

"Mr. and Mrs. MacLachlan?" she greets us with a smile.

I nod, my heart making a familiar flip-flop at the mention of my married name. I can't imagine ever getting tired of hearing it.

"Welcome," she says. "I'm Emma. I'll just need to check your IDs, and then I'll take you straight to your plane."

Andrew and I make quick work of producing our identification, and Emma gestures for us to follow. We walk through a set of automated glass doors and follow her outside, where a fairly large white jet waits not far away. The weathered Union Jack emblem of The Royal Rebels is emblazoned on the plane's tail. Emma stops at the jet stairs leading into the aircraft.

"You can leave your bags here and we'll load them for you," Emma tells us. "Your companion is already onboard."

As if on queue, a voice booms from inside the plane.

"Get up here and hug me, Auntie Scarlet!"

I squeal in delight and run up the stairs, calling, "Thank you, Emma!" behind me. Andrew follows, laughing softly.

I step inside the luxuriously appointed plane and rush to Max, who sets aside a pair of crutches and squashes me in a hug. I squeeze as hard as I can, then pull away to gesture at his knee and the crutches.

"Max, how are you doing? That looks painful."

Marina's brother shrugs his broad shoulders, but his expression is laced with something serious.

"I'm okay," he replies, trying his best to sound nonchalant. "They're calling it a small tear of my meniscus. Luckily, it happened during our last game, so I have until spring to recover."

I nod and settle into one of the seats closest to him. The seating is about a thousand cuts above any commercial aircraft I've ever seen, with plush leather seats that swivel. Andrew and Max give each other what I lovingly call a dude hug, then they settle into their seats.

"So how's married life, you two?" Max asks.

Andrew grins. "Pretty perfect. I highly recommend it."

Max laughs, but there's a kind of sadness about it.

"That sounds nice, actually," he shares. "Between school, sports, and volunteering, I'm usually so busy I don't have time to date. I'm kind of looking forward to this trip."

I reach over and place a hand on his forearm, squeezing gently.

"It'll be good for both of us to have a break."

Andrew reaches over and laces our fingers together.

"And I'll get to spend some quality time with my beautiful wife."

Before I can grab him for a kiss, our pilot comes up the steps.

"Good afternoon, everyone," he says with a grin. "I'm First Officer Gross. Our captain will be along shortly."

We all greet him in unison, and he goes over some brief safety procedures before a woman boards the plane in a similar uniform. She smiles in greeting.

"Hello, friends," she says breezily. "I'm Captain Gross."

I raise my eyebrows and look from the Captain to the First Officer curiously.

She laughs.

"Yes, we're married," she says. "But don't worry, we've never had a marital spat while flying."

The first officer chuckles.

"Just call me Alex," he says as he takes his seat in the cockpit.

The captain points at her seat.

"Are you okay if I leave the door open? It's easier to communicate with you if I need to, but some people prefer it closed."

None of us minds the door open, which is pretty cool. We'll have a unique view that no one gets on a commercial flight. The captain gives us a quick rundown on what to expect on our five-hour flight, then she settles into her seat. We're in the air quickly, and I feel renewed excitement that I'll be reunited with my girlfriends soon.

I catch Max looking wistfully out the window, and I give him a nudge.

"You're looking pretty serious over there, Max."

Max turns in his seat and smiles at me. It's a tired smile, and he suddenly seems older than the twenty-one-year-old he is.

"I'm just tired," he says quietly. "School. Baseball. Coaching. Working part-time. I don't mean to sound like a whiner, but it's been so much to handle."

"You're not whining," I tell him. "Everyone gets tired once in a while."

Andrew leans forward, giving Max a compassionate look.

"Are you still deciding on a major?" he asks.

Max nods. "More pressure. I'm just not sure."

I pat his arm. "You will. Don't rush it."

"My dad is always so certain with everything he does," Max says. "He never struggles with decisions. I wish I were more like him."

I've never met Max's dad, but I've heard good things about him. It's a unique situation, as he and Marina went into foster care when their mother died. Marina was thirteen and Max was nine. They were separated, and Max's foster parents ended up adopting him, so his father isn't Marina's. They never knew their birth father.

"I'm sure he seems like he never struggles with decisions," Andrew chimes in. "But I guarantee that's only what it looks like. Have you talked to him about it?"

Max smirks as if he knows it's something he should probably do, but hasn't yet.

"Maybe when I get back home," he says tiredly. "In a way, I almost think this injury will be good for me. It'll make me slow down for a while."

"I completely understand, Max," I say gently. "Don't get me wrong, I'm very grateful for the break I got when I was offered my home decorating TV show. The show, buying our first home, getting married, trying to settle down."

Max nods and holds a hand up for a high-five.

"Let's commit to letting go and having some fun this weekend."

I smack my hand against his. "Deal."

Max nods his head at Andrew. "How's the fire investigator thing going?"

"Best job ever," Andrew says. "I'm learning a ton, so nothing's boring at this point. I do miss my friends at Engine 14, but I see Jake all the time. I try to stop by the station once or twice a month to say hi."

Max nods solemnly. "Glad you're doing what you love."

Andrew leans forward and squeezes Max on the shoulder.

"Hey, bud," he murmurs. "It'll come to you. One day you'll be grabbing a coffee or just doing something random, and you'll know what you want to do."

"But for now...we rest," I tell him as I spread a blanket out across my lap. "And have a great time with our peeps this weekend."

Max smiles at me and nods. "Sounds good to me."

***

Five hours later, the slow banking of the airplane stirs me from my sleep. I lift my head off Andrew's shoulder to find him already awake. He smiles softly and brings his lips down to mine for a slow, sweet kiss.

"Are we landing?" I ask groggily.

"We're on final approach," he says. "I'm surprised the captain's updates didn't wake you."

I look over at Max, who is still out cold. Poor kid. I know Marina has a great relationship with her brother. Still, I make a mental note to mention his stress level when we're alone. He really seems to need some TLC. I turn back to my handsome husband.

"Did you sleep at all?"

He shrugs adorably. "I took a little catnap. I'm not as worn out as you two."

I reach over and lace our fingers together as the plane banks again. A smattering of lights flicker on the ground below. We're flying into Westchester County Airport, which is nothing like JFK or LaGuardia. I look at my watch. It's nearly ten o'clock at night. Marina said it's only a twenty-minute drive to their home from the airport, and I'm extra grateful for Zach's kind heart and private jet. I'm ready to go right to bed.

Max stirs in his seat, then stretches and looks over at us with a sleepy smile.

"Hello, friends," he says through a yawn. "Are we there yet?"

I nod. "Just about."

"I'm ready for a shower and another nap," he says with a grin. "This whole idea of relaxing and having fun is exhausting."

Andrew and I both laugh, and the captain looks over her shoulder at us.

"We're landing in three minutes, folks. Please be sure those seatbelts are buckled."

I only took mine off to use the bathroom, and then I put it right back on. There's something about flying in airplanes that makes me want to anchor myself to the seat.

Captain Gross expertly maneuvers the plane into position and sets us gently down on the runway. Lots of hugs, a shower, a bed…and maybe a snack are just minutes away. I haven't seen Marina in almost two months because our schedules keep clashing. I see Ashley more often because we live in the same neighborhood, so it's easier for one of us to drop by…and we usually find time to go grab lunch at Nonno's so we can see Merry too.

We taxi for a few minutes, and then the plane stops, and our married pilot and first officer exit the cockpit together.

"I hope you enjoyed your flight," the first officer says.

"It was great," Max says as Andrew and I nod in agreement. "Thanks so much."

The captain opens the aircraft door for us, and we grab our belongings. I double-check for anything left behind, of course, because I'm me. I can't help it. Then we exit the plane after thanking the flying Grosses again.

The stark cold of New York in the fall wakes me right up. It's invigorating. They've already had snow once this year, and there are still traces of it around the edges of the terminal building. Andrew wraps an arm around me as I shiver against the cold, and I smile up at him.

"Isn't this great? It never gets this cold in San Francisco."

He kisses me sweetly, but doesn't reply. A dark SUV pulls up as we walk away from the plane, and an airport employee pulls our bags out of the cargo hold. Max grabs his, and Andrew takes ours as the driver exits the vehicle.

"Welcome to New York state," the older gentleman says with a polite smile. "Let's get your bags in the back and get you on your way. It's warmer in the car."

In less than two minutes, we're all seated in the back of the SUV. How will I ever go back to commercial travel after being spoiled like this? Private jet. Car service. Yes, please!

Max frowns next to me. "I need a snack."

I grin in the dark confines of the car. "If I know your sister, she'll have something out for us. She's so excited for this weekend, we might die from overeating by the time it's over."

Max laughs. "I'm really looking forward to some sister time. I've missed her."

"I know she's missed you, too."

The rest of our trip to Zach and Marina's estate passes quietly. We all watch out the windows as dark woods turn into the charming town of Sleepy Hollow. Since it's so late, nothing much is open, and things are fairly still. But I can make out sweet little shop fronts, restaurants, and a fairly large sculpture of the Headless Horseman as our driver navigates us closer to our friends. I duck my head to get a better view out the window as we pass a church, then I gasp and point.

"That's the Old Dutch Church," I tell my companions. "From the story of Sleepy Hollow."

Max grins at me. "Did you read the story before this trip or something?"

I laugh. "I did! I've wanted to do it for a while. Thankfully, it's just a short story and not a huge book, or I wouldn't have been able to do it until we're done filming my show."

"What did you think of it?" Max asks. "I read it before my first trip here as well."

I sit back in my seat and nestle into Andrew's side.

"I loved it. It's so charmingly written. Washington Irving must have really loved this area, and it shows in the way he describes it."

The view out the windows turns back to darkened woods as the car winds down a quiet road. I keep watching, as if I might look into those woods and see the Headless Horseman just waiting for us to get close enough.

"Here we are," our driver says as he pulls up to a massive iron gate.

The gate opens automatically, and the car pulls slowly up the curved driveway, under a stone arch, and around to the side of the massive estate.

Andrew opens the door and gets out, then offers me his hand as I scoot toward the door. We both stretch as the driver moves to open the trunk.

The large, wooden front door opens, and Marina and Zach come out to greet us. I run to my friend and envelop her in a hug. It's indescribably wonderful to be back with my best friends, and I'm so grateful for this chance to reconnect.

"Welcome, my friend," Marina says as she pulls back. "I'm sure you're pretty exhausted. We have food ready in case you're hungry, but I can also show you straight to your room if you'd rather just crash."

Andrew steps in next to me with his arms open.

"I need my hug before I grab the bags, Marina."

"Andrew, welcome," Marina says, with a laugh.

"And yes to the snacks," I tell my friend just as Zach pulls me into a hug.

"Hey, gorgeous," Zach growls as he squeezes me tight, making me laugh under my breath.

"Hey, rockstar," I answer back. "You taking good care of our girl?"

I hear the clicking of Max's crutches, and I know he's heading for his sister. Andrew sidles up next to me with our bag and Max's as well.

After greetings and hugs are exchanged all around, we're ushered up the three broad stone steps to the front door. Once inside the large foyer, Zach confirms which bag is Max's, and he heads up a beautiful jack-and-jill style staircase to drop it in his room.

"Let's get you fed," Marina says in a musical tone, motioning for us to follow her.

We walk through the great room, which is beautifully decorated in shades of cream, gray, and pops of turquoise. A wall of windows is at the back, overlooking part of the backyard and the woods beyond it. It's dark outside, so I can't see much past the backyard lighting. We follow Marina through an archway into a large, beautifully appointed kitchen with a huge island. An island that is covered in a very fun-looking skeleton charcuterie board. Plates and napkins are set out, as well as a small bucket with cold drinks.

"Marina, that is creepy and tasty-looking," I tell my friend as I grab a plate. "Well done."

Marina laughs. "The others will tell you tomorrow that they also got the skeleton charcuterie at cocktail hour, so I want to assure you this is not leftover from five hours ago. This is fresh, I promise."

I nudge her playfully. "Like you have to tell us that."

Max plops down on a barstool and grabs a plate. He's such a big guy. His long arms have no trouble reaching any part of the skeleton. I wait until he's done dishing his own plate up and hand him mine.

"Can you throw a few olives and some cheese on that?"

He laughs and does as I ask, but he heaps way too much food on my plate by the time he sets it down in front of me. Athletes have much bigger stomachs than interior designers.

Andrew grabs a spot next to me with his own plate, and I find myself stifling a yawn before I get the first bite to my mouth. Zach's gravelly laugh echoes through the kitchen.

"You've had a long day, guys," he says. "We'll get you tucked in soon."

"I'm just glad to be here and officially unplugged from work," I tell them. "No cameras following me around. No having to do thing three times because I forgot to stand in the right place or someone coughed in the background."

I see something moving outside the French doors that lead to the backyard, and I gasp when I realize it's Ashley. She rushes through the door, and I bolt out of my seat to get to her. We crash together in a crazy, laughter-fueled hug.

"Oh, I missed you!" she cries out, and I squeeze her harder because I missed her too.

When we finally let each other go, it's only to discover that Marina has moved close enough to grab, so we pull her into the middle, and now we're in a three-way hug. The only thing missing is Merry.

"I suppose Merry's asleep?" I ask without letting go.

"She worked so hard today," Marina says. "I'm sure she—"

"Well, if it isn't my sisters from other misters," Merry's voice sounds from right behind me.

I gasp and spin around, and now my entire world is perfect. Absolutely perfect. The four of us girlfriends. Sisters by choice. Back together again for the first time in months. The heaviness of all the change and turmoil of the past several months lifts instantly, and my throat clogs with emotion.

"I really missed you guys," I croak through happy tears.

We just stand there, holding onto each other, for who knows how long. I'm vaguely aware of Andrew, Zach, and Max chatting amongst themselves. Nothing matters outside the little bubble of our happy reunion right now. Finally, we begin to let go...if only so we can step back and actually look at each other.

Merry snorts at me. "Only you could look perfect after a full work day and a five-hour flight."

I hold a hand up to halt her praise. "If it makes you feel any better, I'm pretty sure I forgot something. I won't be sure of what until I unpack."

Marina waves a hand. "You can borrow my car if you need to pick up anything in town. Don't even worry about it."

"I'll definitely be doing that in the morning," Max chimes in.

Zach raises his eyebrows.

"Forgot something? I don't believe it. You're too much like your sister."

"All my socks," Max confesses with a tired grin. "I was already at the airport when I realized it."

Marina eyes her brother with mock suspicion. "Maybe it was subconscious."

Max gives her a look like he knows exactly where she's going.

"Sometimes it's just about forgetting the socks, sis."

"And sometimes it's not," she replies cryptically.

I'm curious, but far too tired to investigate further. I don't even bother to stifle the yawn that rolls out of me. We visit for a few more minutes before it becomes painfully evident that some of us are too tired to keep going. We all bid each other goodnight before Marina walks Andrew and me to the guest cottage, and Zach makes sure Max is settled upstairs. For the first time in a long time, I won't be waking up at the crack of dawn, rushing through my morning. I don't think there's another person on the planet more excited about sleeping in than I am.

***

"You know what? You're a guy," I tell Andrew with a smirk on my face. "And guys just don't understand these things."

To my delight, Andrew pulls me into his lap on the sofa in the quaint little living room in our guest cottage. I wrap my arms around him and place a light kiss right on one of his dimples.

"The goal was to relax this weekend," he reminds me.

"Calm down, Superman. Just because I need to run into town to get some eyeliner and a few things doesn't mean I'm not going to relax."

His watchful eyes roam over my face.

"You look beautiful without a stitch of makeup."

Love floods through me from head to toe. This man is my everything. That earns him a real kiss, which makes my toes curl and threatens to make me late for meeting Max up at the main house.

When I realized that I'd forgotten not only eyeliner but also my eyelash curler, I went through all of my belongings twice and made sure I hadn't forgotten anything else. Then I ran straight up to the house with the intention of telling Marina not to let Max leave without me. Instead, I found Max and Marina both…adorably sitting at the kitchen island with bowls of cereal, having a much-needed brother/sister catch-up. I didn't want to intrude, so I agreed to meet Max back up at the house in an hour. I've spent that hour making out with my husband like it's our first date, and now I need to get going.

"I appreciate the fact that you think I'm beautiful no matter what," I say as I wriggle off his lap and wrestle myself out of his grip. "But I need eyeliner and you're not going to stop me."

Andrew laughs and shakes his head. "I still don't get it."

"For one thing, my costume won't look right without it."

I laugh out loud at the look of unabashed confusion on his face. "You're a bumblebee…"

"Yes. But a sexy bumblebee."

Andrew sits back against the couch with a chuckle.

"The sexiest. Okay, hurry up so you can come back to me."

I grin. "I will. See you up at the house for brunch?"

He nods. "Ten-thirty. Yes, ma'am."

I blow him a kiss, grab my purse, and step out the door. Walking up the path to the house, I let my gaze wander around the beautiful landscaping back here. There's a flower garden, which looks like a miniaturized version of the gorgeous, manicured garden at Zach's ancestral home in England. There's also a well-maintained vegetable garden before the path inclines, and I'm in the swimming pool area. I wave at Marina, who's watching me through the French doors as I hit the patio.

Max jingles Marina's car keys at me. "Ready?"

"Ready!" I reply, then turn quickly to Marina. "We won't be long. Do you need anything?"

Marina shakes her head. "Nope. The caterers will be here any minute, and they're doing all the work this weekend so I can have fun with everyone else. I'm good."

I give her a hug goodbye and jump ahead of Max to open the door for him since he's on crutches.

"Are you driving or am I?" I ask.

"I didn't hurt my driving leg, Scarlet. You worried?" he teases.

I follow him across the circular driveway to a set of garages positioned off to one side of the house, near the woods.

"Not a bit, you brat."

We both laugh, and before long, we're turning onto the road in Marina's SUV.

"So Marina said there's a drug store in town?"

Max nods, and I feel like he looks a little too excited for a guy who just needs to buy socks.

"Wallaby's," he says. "Great little store. Since it's a fairly small town, they stock some things you wouldn't find in a traditional drug store. They even have an old-fashioned soda fountain. It's been in business for over a hundred years, it's pretty cool."

"Cool."

We're quiet as Max drives us through a beautiful spot of woods, then the town begins to take shape. I see the Old Dutch Church again, and the sculpture of the Headless Horseman. The road narrows, and soon quaint little shops are everywhere. Max pulls into an empty spot on the curb and parks.

As I get out, I can't help but notice Max trying to look inside the drug store. I ignore it and step onto the curb as he gets out and pulls his crutches out of the back seat. As he gets close to the door, I hold it open for him, and he smiles his thanks.

Once inside, I head off to the makeup section for my items. I quickly find what I need, but notice they have a very cool Halloween section in the store, and I head that way to check it out.

"Oh, Max, hi!" a very sweet, young, decidedly feminine voice cries out.

Hmm. Interesting.

"Hey, Gabi," Max replies. "It's nice to see you."

I smirk to myself. Forgotten socks indeed. Now I understand Marina's teasing last night.

"You're hurt," she says with concern. "Are you okay? What happened?"

"I'm fine, it's no big deal," he says in a very tough guy voice. "Torn meniscus, but it happened at the end of the season. How've you been?"

She makes a sputtering sound.

"Same old news, different day," she says with the air of a girl who's tired of small-town living. "My lack of a life update is somewhat depressing when you think about it."

"There's nothing about you that's depressing."

Oh, hello.

This is getting very interesting.

"You're sweet to say that," she replies. "I just can't seem to make a difference lately."

Um. Hey, girl, you're making a difference to the handsome future baseball star standing in front of you. Pay attention.

"Okay, let's work the problem," he says quietly.

Boy, does he sound like Marina when he talks like this.

"What are the obstacles?"

66

She lets out a puff of air. "Same as always. Money."

"Okay, I get it," he says gently. "Dogs or cats this time?"

She laughs softly. "I'm actually trying to start a rescue for large breed dogs, I'm just coming up a little short on funding. But there might be a solution."

"Yeah? That sounds promising."

I hear a soft laugh.

"In a small town like this, there's only so much funding I can get," she says. "I have the land, thanks to my grandpa. He's living with my parents now and, well, that's a whole other story. I've tapped out all my resources, and I'm still about four thousand dollars short of what I need to really get it started."

"That's a lot of money."

"Especially for me," she says. "Once I finish college, I still have vet school, so I'm already broke. Working here part time only covers my basic expenses."

"And I know you have a soft spot for the really big doggos," Max says in a voice laced with humor.

I can barely stand to stay in this aisle. I want to meet this girl. Maybe I can help things along. Although it wasn't too long ago when I would have killed anyone who even tried to introduce me to a guy. Max might not take kindly to any interference.

"So you said there might be a solution?"

"Yeah, but it sounds so stupid," she says, laughing nervously. "I'm embarrassed to tell you."

"Come on," Max says in a flirty, coaxing voice. "You can tell me."

"Have you ever been to the Headless Horseman?"

"The pub?" Max asks. "Once with my brother-in-law, yeah."

"They're having a karaoke contest tonight," she shares. "And the grand prize is five thousand dollars for the charity of your choice."

"Oh," Max replies. "Do you sing?"

She laughs out loud.

"No, I can't participate because technically I'm the charity," she says. "It's my rescue, and I can't sing, anyway. My sister and her friend were going to compete for me, but now her friend isn't sure she can make it. It's kind of falling apart."

"Hmm..."

Uh-oh. I have to put my hand over my mouth to keep from laughing out loud. I can almost hear Max's lovesick brain thinking. He's got a sister who can sing. And her three friends. And his world-famous brother-in-law. Almost everyone staying on the estate can sing, except for Max and my sweet Andrew.

"I can't promise anything," Max begins, "but I might be able to help."

"What?" the girl gasps. "How?"

He laughs nervously.

"I don't want to say because I don't want to get your hopes up. What time is the contest tonight?"

"It's after the Halloween costume contest, so it's at ten o'clock."

More nervous laughter.

"Okay, that might actually work."

"Max," she says softly. "You don't have to go to any trouble for me. I'll figure it out."

Silence. Just as I'm wondering what's happening, he clears his throat nervously.

"Gabi, I know you don't know me very well," he says in the sweetest tone. "And maybe that'll never change because we live so far apart. But...I'd like to help if I can."

More silence.

"And that's so sweet of you. I guess I just don't understand why."

He clears his throat again.

"I'm, um," Max stammers. "Because I think you're really sweet. And I love that you want to help animals so much. Sorry if that makes things awkward. Since you don't know me that well."

Now she clears her throat.

"I think that's one of the sweetest things anyone's ever said to me, Max."

Oh my gosh…I'm going to explode, I'm so excited. These two are so cute!

"Just don't get your hopes set too high because I actually might not be able to pull this off at all," he says. "And the last thing I want to do is disappoint you."

She giggles.

Giggles.

"Max, I can't imagine you ever disappointing me."

I can't contain myself anymore. I bust out in a happy dance around in a little circle. They are so freaking cute. I have to find a way to help this along. There has to be a way, and that starts with me getting back to the house so I can tell Marina about her brother's little secret crush on Gabi.

Chapter 5

Andrew

Something's definitely up, but I'm having too much fun watching Scarlet to tell her to come over here and fill me in. I came up to the house at ten this morning to see if I could help with anything. Spoiler alert: Marina and her catering team are a well-oiled machine. No help needed.

My curiosity started when Scarlet came jogging into the house, excitedly searching for Marina. She found Marina in the kitchen with me, Jimmy, Beth, and Ashley. Marina was promptly grabbed on the arm by my sweet wife and dragged into the pantry. The rest of us exchanged curious looks, but said nothing.

While Marina and Scarlet were having their not-so-secret meeting in the pantry, Rick and Zach came in and joined us. Now here comes Max, moving more slowly because of the crutches. He pulls up a stool at the kitchen island and nods at me.

"Did Scarlet make it in okay?" he asks. "She said she really had to use the bathroom."

Hmm. And yet my beautiful bride did not, in fact, sprint to the bathroom. She grabbed Marina and pulled her into the pantry. I nod at Max as the pantry door swings open and Marina sticks her head out.

"Zach?" she calls out sweetly. "Can you come and help me with something?"

Zach excuses himself from the group and heads for the pantry, where he's also dragged inside. What. Is. Happening? I look around, and no one else has noticed that the pantry has suddenly become a hot spot for…I'm not sure what. My investigator instincts are tingling, and I sit back in my seat to watch the show.

The pantry door opens, and Zach exits with Marina not far behind. She joins those of us who have taken seats around the island while Zach pulls Rick off to the side. They're obviously bringing Rick into the fold.

Now Sam and Bella join us, but they're chatting with Jimmy and Beth. Max, who is eyeing Marina like he has something to say, thinks better of it when Ashley appears and gives her a hug.

"Everything okay, bud?" I ask Max instinctively.

Since Scarlet came running into the house ahead of Max and went straight for his sister, I'm thinking this might have something to do with him. Max nods.

"Really looking forward to just chilling out and having fun this weekend."

"Me too," I tell him. "The hockey game will be fun."

"Yeah, it will," he agrees. "I guess Marina's got all the ladies doing something different, and then we're coming back here for dinner. I was thinking I might have something fun for us to do after that."

I blink, and Zach and Rick have joined us.

"What are you gents talking about?"

Over Zach's shoulder, I get a glimpse of Scarlet tiptoeing out of the pantry, finally. Max seems excited to share.

"Well, yeah, actually, I was just telling Andrew I have a great idea for something we could do after dinner."

"Oh, cool," Rick says. "What is it?"

My eyes are stuck on Zach, who is great on stage, but his acting is terrible. He's excited about Max's idea, and it's all over his face. Max doesn't seem to notice as he shifts in his seat.

"There's a karaoke contest at The Headless Horseman pub tonight," he tells us. "It's a charity thing. I was thinking it'd be fun to help."

Both Rick and Zach do a terrible job of looking surprised by the suggestion. They totally know. I stifle a laugh as Scarlet runs over and joins our little group, slipping an arm around my waist.

"Hey guys, what's up?"

Zach looks at Scarlet with an excited expression.

"Max was just telling us there's a karaoke contest for charity in town tonight that he wants to do."

I may be biased, but Scarlet is a much better actress.

"Oh, that does sound fun!"

I realize Marina is missing, and I'm sure she's bringing the others in on the worst-kept secret ever. It's fun to be a spectator in this, and I'm glad I can't sing. They won't ask me for help.

Max pulls a piece of paper out of his back pocket and unfolds it. It's a flyer advertising the event, and the whole group quiets as we all lean over and read. It's Halloween costume night, so there's a lot about that. The karaoke contest begins at ten tonight. Contestants must sing two songs: one rock, one country. Several businesses, including the pub, are sponsoring the contest and the five-thousand-dollar prize that goes to the winner's favorite charity.

Zach tilts his head. "Well, it is for charity. We couldn't do it otherwise. It wouldn't be right."

Max looks up at his brother-in-law with such hope in his eyes, I want to give the guy a hug.

"So you might do it? Really? Because that would be so awesome."

Zach grins at Max and wiggles his eyebrows.

"I might. But you have to tell me what's in it for you, Max."

Max laughs self-consciously.

"My friend Gabi could use that prize money for her animal rescue."

Rick grins at Max. "Gabi, huh?"

Max rolls his eyes at Rick.

"Yeah, she's a girl," Max blurts. "And yeah, she's pretty. Gorgeous, actually. And so nice."

Zach's eyes shine with brotherly love as he slaps a hand on Max's broad shoulder.

"I'm in, Max," he says. "On one condition. You have to sing with us."

Max's eyes nearly bulge out of their sockets.

"Wrong sibling, Zach. Marina's got the pipes. I can't sing at all."

Rick laughs and shakes his head.

"We can't be up there without you," he explains. "Gabi needs to see you up there fighting for this prize right alongside us. Otherwise, you're just some guy who called in a favor."

Max doesn't look convinced.

"Relax, brother," Zach tells him. "We're The Royal Rebels. We're so loud on stage, no one's going to hear you or Andrew."

I jolt in my seat. "Pardon?"

Zach nods emphatically. "You're in the family now, Andrew. We can't let Max down."

Max turns to me with a hopeful expression.

"Oh, c'mon...don't make me be the only one up there who can't sing. Please?"

I don't even have to look at Scarlet to know there's an unspoken plea in those beautiful eyes of hers. This is so ridiculous.

"Okay, sure. I'll do it."

I'm such a sucker, mostly for my wife, but also for this group of friends who have embraced me as one of their own. With every outing, every party…they're becoming more and more like family to me.

"All right, quick reality check," Zach says under his breath. "Bella? Where's Hella Bella?"

Bella comes running from somewhere in the house, yelling, "Here!"

"We want to do something crazy, and we need you to be okay with it," Zach says with a wide grin.

Bella nods. "Hit me."

"Karaoke contest at the pub tonight for charity," he begins, ticking items off on his fingers as he speaks. "Winner gets five thousand dollars for the charity of their choice. We're in it to win it because Max wants to impress a girl."

"Hey!" Max interjects.

We all look at him as if to say *Don't even bother to argue.* He grins and shakes his head in embarrassment.

Bella nods again. "Okay, let's think this through."

Ashley steps in. "What are we thinking through?"

Rick starts whispering in her ear to bring her up to speed.

"How are they *not* going to recognize you guys?" Bella says. "You're the freaking Royal Rebels."

"It's also Halloween costume night," comes Zach's reply.

"Do all your costumes cover your faces?" she asks.

"Mine does," Zach says. He looks around at the other Rebels.

"Mine too," Rick pipes in.

Jimmy and Sam, who've been filled in on the plan during this chaos, both nod. Everyone looks at me.

"Why are you asking me? I'm not famous."

Zach lets out a gravelly laugh.

"Actually, I might not be able to get up on stage in my costume," Rick says cryptically. "I'll need to come up with something else."

Zach thinks for a moment. "Why don't we just go as cowboys? The whole lot. I have my cowboy hat collection, which I can loan out. We all have jeans. That seems the least trouble."

Everyone nods in agreement.

"We'll put bandanas over our faces," Rick adds. "It would muffle a normal voice, but we're loud enough. It'll be fine."

"Right. Okay, Bella," Zach says. "Are we okay to proceed with Operation Max Gets The Girl?"

"Hey!" Max objects.

I wrap an arm around his shoulders and give him a shake until he laughs.

"I still have questions," Bella replies. "What are you singing?"

Zach looks at Rick, Jimmy, and Sam.

"Is it too obvious if we sing a Rebels song? Our faces will be covered."

We all look around at each other. Finally, I shrug.

"We want to win, right? No one sounds more like The Royal Rebels than you guys."

"And what happens if you're discovered?" Bella asks. "What do we do if they figure out you're The Royal Rebels?"

Zach scoffs. "First of all, if we win, I have a plan. But I'm not going to share."

Rick laughs. "He's going rogue again."

"If they realize it's us before we win, we play it off as just having fun for charity…which we're doing, so it's not a lie. Simple."

Bella scrunches her face as she thinks through every possible scenario. As the band's manager, it's her job to think ahead and protect them from bad publicity. Finally, she nods at the guys.

"Okay, I say go for it."

Max sits up straighter. "Yeah?"

"Yeah. But what are you guys singing?"

"It can't be a ballad," Jimmy says. "We want to get the crowd riled up."

"Highway to Love," Sam suggests.

The guys agree on that for the rock song we're singing.

"And the country song?" Bella asks.

For some unknown reason, all eyes turn to Rick. He grins and claps his hands together, rubbing them together like he's concocting a diabolical plan. His eyes find Ashley's.

"May I suggest T-R-O-U-B-L-E by Travis Tritt?" he says without taking his eyes off her. A low laugh is her only response.

"Oh, I love that song," Zach says. "If you're doing lead vocals, I'm in." Rick nods. "Absolutely."

"Okay, but seriously, how are Andrew and I not going to suck up there?"

"Hey!" I object teasingly.

Max nudges me. "Sorry, dude."

"It'll be easy, Max," Zach says matter-of-factly. "We'll put you and Andrew at one mic together. You guys can be backup singers."

Max and I exchange looks. That doesn't sound too bad, actually.

With all that settled, Marina gets us all moving toward the incredible brunch buffet that's been set out for us in the small dining room. Apparently, there's another dining room where we're eating. I can't imagine living in a house with so many rooms.

I grab two plates and hand one to Scarlet. She stands on her toes and brings her lips up to my ear.

"Thank you so much, baby," she whispers. "Are you really okay doing this?"

I give her a reassuring smile.

"I'm okay, Nix. Are you going to give me the whole scoop later?"

She squeezes my arm. "You better believe it. Let's run back to the cottage for a few minutes before you go to the hockey game."

I give her a little fist bump, and she winks at me. That's all it takes for my gut to somersault. I'd do anything for the slightest hint of a smile from this beautiful creature next to me. I guess that's evident by

76

the fact that I'm about to get on a stage in a bar and pretend I can sing in front of a bunch of drunk strangers.

***

Two hours later, the car service Zach hired drops all the guys off at the sports venue where the local AHL hockey team plays. Nicknamed The Valley because of the Hudson River Valley nearby, it's pretty impressive. Since we're guests of Zach and Marina's neighbor, and he owns the team, I'm not sure why I'm surprised when we're led up to the VIP entrance.

As we're ushered to our seats, I go over my conversation with Scarlet after brunch. She filled me in on the Max and Gabi situation. If I wasn't in before, I definitely am now. Max seems like such a good guy, and I understand the pressure he's putting on himself to find his place in the world. It's vital for him to feel supported right now, so that's what we're going to do.

I bump him on the shoulder as we descend into the arena.

"Why are you so quiet?"

Max pulls an earbud out of his ear and shows it to me. He is only wearing one, and I give him a confused look.

"I want to be able to hear you guys and enjoy the game, but I'm also trying to memorize the lyrics to the songs we have to sing tonight."

I laugh out loud and give him a single pat on the back.

"It's going to be fine, Max," I tell him. "The Rebels are professional performers. No one's going to be looking at us."

"Normally, I'd say that's a good thing, but I kind of *want* Gabi to look at me. At least some of the time."

Right. Solid point. I want Max to have a great weekend and feel supported. I throw him a quick wink.

"I have an idea. Back me up."

I nudge Zach, Rick, and everyone within nudging distance as we file into our row of seats, which is right up against the glass. They all turn to me.

"So I'm all in on the karaoke thing," I tell them. "But since Max and I are the only two in the group who aren't professional singers and aren't used to being on stage, can we squeeze a rehearsal in somehow?"

Zach lets out a gravelly laugh as the guys nod in unison.

"Absolutely, mate," he says, then he looks over at Max. "We won't let you go on stage without knowing what you're doing, brother. Let's have fun and watch the game, then we'll head straight back and have a rehearsal. Okay?"

The tension that rolls off of Max is nearly palpable, and I feel like I've had a small part in making tonight a success. Hopefully, it will be a success. Please.

We all sit in our seats, and I notice Max putting his earbuds away. I give him a nod.

"We got this, Max. We're gonna win the contest and you're gonna get the girl."

His face brightens into a grin.

"That's a lot of confidence coming from the other guy who can't sing, but I love it."

"Can you dance?"

His eyes bulge. "I am not dancing on stage, dude."

I laugh out loud.

"No, that's not what I'm saying. We can't stand at the mic like statues. We have to at least pop a knee once in a while."

He groans.

"Oh, man…"

"Scarlet gave me some tips. We're gonna be fine."

"Yeah? What tips?"

I stand up and face Max, gesturing at my feet.

"We're gonna stand with our feet apart and just kind of bounce to the beat while we do our thing at the mic."

I show him what I'm talking about, and I get a few moves in before two hockey players slam into the glass right behind me. I jump about three feet because I'm not paying attention to the warm-ups going on out there. All the guys break into hysterical laughter.

"They were distracted by your sweet moves, Andrew!" Sam teases.

"Truth," I say as I sit down and grin at Max. "Be confident in all things. Even if you don't know what on earth you're doing."

Max and I both laugh. I turn my focus on the players skating around the ice. The local AHL team we're here to see, The Horsemen, is playing a team from Orange County, California called the Surfers. I'm not aware of a big hockey vibe in a place where it doesn't snow, so my money's on The Horsemen. A lot of these guys are local, and they would have grown up with hockey. That's my theory, anyway.

Max shakes his head as he watches the players go through their warm-ups.

"Are you a hockey fan, Max?" I ask.

"Fan? Yes. I could never play it. I can't imagine playing any sport with knives strapped to my feet while I flail around on the ice."

I laugh out loud at that one.

"Same."

A tall, disgustingly good-looking man walks over to the opposite end of our row, where Zach is sitting. Zach immediately stands and greets him, then begins introducing everyone down the line. We each wave and say hello as we're introduced to Jack Bixley, owner of the Headless Horsemen team.

Zach told us a little about him on the way over to the stadium. Wealthy guy, obviously. He also owns some tech companies, including a social media app called ShutterBug that Scarlet uses. He's super nice. Big fan of The Royal Rebels. Max and I are too far away to hear the conversation, so we focus on getting to know the players on the team.

"This guy right here," Max says as he points to a player whizzing past.

"Number eleven. Dean Stauber. They call him Mean Dean because he gets in so many fights. He's fun to watch."

"Have you been watching number twenty-seven? Mason?" I ask. "I didn't know anyone could do the things on skates that he's doing just during a warm-up. The guy's amazing."

"Oh yeah, he's good," Max replies. "I've been to games with Zach and Marina before. I like him a lot."

Zach and Rick come down the row, taking drink orders from the guys.

"You guys want some extra hands?" I offer.

"Yeah, we can help," Max adds, prompting us all to look pointedly at his crutches.

"Well, I can go with you. Stretch my good leg."

We laugh and get up, following them to the closest concession stand, where Zach refuses to let any of us pay for our drinks. While we wait for the order, Zach fills us in on what they were talking about.

"I told Jack about karaoke tonight," he begins. "He won't tell anyone it's us, but I wanted to run it by him to see if he thinks it would spark a negative reaction that the Rebels did something like this. He agreed with me that it'll be fine, especially since it's for charity - but Marina and I plan to donate five thousand dollars to all the contestants' charities."

"Wow, really?" an awestruck Max says.

Zach taps his chest. "Feels better in here, whether they figure out we're The Royal Rebels or not. If we do win, we'd be using our professional talent to beat amateurs at a charity event. That's not cool. If we do it this way, everyone wins."

Max shrugs. "Well, if you're doing that, do we really need to get on stage and—"

"Yep," Zach interrupts, holding up a hand. "Sorry, brother, but I'm not about to rob you of this experience."

Max and I exchange puzzled looks.

"What experience, exactly?" Max asks.

"Pulling out all the stops to impress a girl," Zach replies. He wiggles his eyebrows at Max. "Women go crazy for it. She'll fall in love with you on the spot."

Max laughs out loud and pulls Zach in for a bro hug.

"Not likely, Zach, but I appreciate your confidence in me."

We gather all the drink orders, along with two huge buckets of popcorn, and descend the stairs with Max leading the way.

"Wouldn't it be funny if some other group kicked our butts?" Rick says with a laugh.

Zach nods. "Even better if they do it with a Rebels song. But don't worry, Max. If someone beats us, Marina and I will still donate to Gabi's rescue."

"Best brother-in-law ever," Max says as he sits and puts his crutches aside.

I hand him his soda, then take mine out of the carrier Zach is holding. He tells us to keep a bucket of popcorn on our end, then he and Rick head down to their seats and distribute the other drinks and popcorn.

"So tell me about this girl," I prompt Max. "I get the feeling this isn't someone you just met today?"

Max laughs softly. "No, I think I met her about six months ago. Marina invited me to come hang out for the weekend, and I forgot to pack socks, so she took me to Wallaby's to get some."

I nod and throw some popcorn in my mouth, content to let Max do all the talking.

"I was trying to hurry, and I couldn't find socks. She was stocking some stuff on an aisle, and I asked her for help," Max explains. "She had her back to me, and when she turned around I was... Well, I was so distracted with how pretty she was, I totally forgot what I was at the store for."

We both laugh. I understand this feeling well. I lost count of how many cups of tea I let go cold at the coffee house after Scarlet walked in, and I couldn't focus anymore. She commanded all my attention just by walking into the room. She still does.

"We talked a little bit, but I couldn't get up the nerve to ask her out," he continues. "I was only here for the weekend. Why would she want to go out with someone who doesn't even live here?"

"What did you talk about that first time?"

"She has a soft spot for animals," he replies. "And she'd found a litter of kittens she was trying to find homes for. She worked me hard trying to get me to take a kitten, but of course, I couldn't take one."

The lights begin to dim in the rink, and cheers begin to erupt in the crowd. Players gradually make their way off the ice.

"So what's different now?" I ask him gently. "You still don't live here."

Max's expression is wistful as he shrugs. "I don't know," he says. "I think of her a lot. Sometimes I see something that reminds me of her, and I wish I could text her about it. And I do come back here and visit Marina and Zach, so it's not like I'll never return. There's something about her. She's..."

"Special," I finish for him, giving him a knowing grin.

That's what Scarlet was for me from the moment we met.

Max nods. "Special."

The team's cheerleaders come skating out of the tunnel, holding lighted pumpkins on poles as the fans cheer. The rink darkens further, and spotlights begin moving all over the ice.

"Well, this is going to be an interesting and fun day," I say with a grin. "We're about to enjoy a hockey game, and then we have to go back to the estate so we can rehearse with The Royal Rebels. Who would've thought?"

Max laughs out loud.

"Right? So crazy. And amazing."

The game gets officially started when we stand for the national anthem. Once that's done, the players waste no time getting in skirmishes over the puck. A player on the opposing team hammers Dyson Duke, number 64, against the glass pretty bad. Duke gives as good as he gets, and then Stauber jumps into the mayhem. I've been to a few hockey games before, but I've never been in seats like these. The action is incredible. Max and I are yelling our heads off and having a great time.

By the first period intermission, the Horsemen are up by two goals, and the energy buzz in the stadium feels electric. Max and I decide to take a quick restroom break, and we find Jack Bixley standing on our side of the row when we return to our seats. He's chatting with Sam and Jimmy. He steps out as we approach so Max can get in with his crutches.

"Thanks, man," Max tells him as he sits.

I remain standing and shake Jack's hand.

"These seats are insane," I tell Jack. "Thank you so much."

"Glad you like them," he replies. "Can I get you guys anything? How'd you hurt yourself, Max?"

Max points to his knee. "That is a torn meniscus, Jack."

"Ouch. I've done that. It was really painful. Will you get to play baseball next year?"

"All the team docs say yes, I just have to take it easy right now. Physical therapy, all that."

Jack nods and pats Max on the shoulder.

"Okay, good luck tonight, kid. I'll be rooting for you from the bar."

Max nearly shoots out of his seat.

"You're going? You're kidding me."

Jack lets out a hearty laugh.

"Are you kidding? The Rebels on a super secret karaoke mission? I wouldn't miss this for the world."

Max lets out a nervous laugh as Jack heads back to wherever he's sitting. I nudge Max with my elbow.

"You okay?"

He swallows. Hard.

"This is turning out to be a bigger deal than I thought it would be."

"No, c'mon," I tell him, trying to make my tone light and nonchalant. "It feels like a big deal because you're nervous about Gabi and you're not used to getting up on stage. That's normal. Look at the positive side of it. We're going to have a blast. You'll be with me, and I don't know what I'm doing either."

Max focuses on his shoes as he listens to my words, nodding.

"And don't forget the best part."

I raise my eyebrows, waiting for him to elaborate.

"At the end of the night, whether we win or not, Gabi will have the money she needs to start her rescue."

A disgustingly lovesick grin grows across Max's face, and I burst out laughing. The guy has it bad, that's for sure.

"Oh, hey," Max says, nudging my elbow. "You're gonna miss the Horseman."

I frown at him and then look where he's looking. The Zamboni machine is driving across the ice, refreshing it for the next round, and the driver is dressed in full Headless Horseman regalia. I do a double-take as soon as I see him, then watch the entire stadium erupt in cheers and applause. He has a light-up pumpkin in his hand that he's pretending to throw at fans. I sit back in my seat as laughter bubbles up. This town is so cool.

***

Hours later, the Rebels, Max, and I all pile out of the car when we get to the estate. Scarlet and the other ladies are all doing something in town, I'm not sure what, and so we have time to get together and work out how the karaoke thing is going to go. If someone other than Max asked me how I feel, I'd tell them I'm super unexcited about this, but I'm determined to support Max. He's a good guy, and Zach is right. Every man should go through a little ridiculousness for the woman he cares for. So I'm supporting Max, and maybe my woman will melt a little over the fact that I'm making myself look ridiculous, too.

Once we grab drinks in the kitchen, we head down the massive hallway, past the library, and into Zach's music room. Wow. There's a grand piano in one corner and a drum kit in another. Several very expensive-looking guitars sit around on stands. The walls are painted a rich dark blue, and there are more guitars mounted on the walls in glass cases. On the opposite wall, there's a light-up trophy case with at least six World Music Awards inside. I don't want to stare. Pretty sure I saw some music video awards as well. I'm desperately trying to look cool, but I'm getting a little starstruck.

"Right," Zach says as he motions for us to sit on the two cream-colored sofas facing each other in the middle of the room. "Gents, we have a singular purpose tonight. Help Max get the girl."

Max's face turns three shades of red as the guys all pat him on the back and tease him a little. We all shuffle around until we all have a spot to sit.

"Tell us about her," Rick says as he leans over and puts his beer on the coffee table between us.

"Um, I don't know," he begins quietly. "Gabi's just so sweet. She loves animals, and she's working really hard in school so she can be a vet. She's pretty, of course, but she has the best laugh."

"Aww!" Sam teases. "Maxy's in love!"

Zach kicks at Sam with a gravelly laugh. "Knock it off, Sammy."

"I can take the teasing, Zach, it's cool," Max says quickly. "I just don't want to look like an idiot up there."

Jimmy grins. "We're all idiots for love."

"Okay, yeah, but there's looking like an idiot and then there's *looking like an idiot*."

Zach nods. "We've got this, baby brother. I'll sing the lead on 'Highway to Love' and Rick's taking the lead on the Travis Tritt cover. This is easy peasy. Ready for rehearsal?"

I watch a moment of panic fly across Max's face, so I smack my hand on his shoulder and smile.

"Let's do this."

Max takes a deep breath and nods as Sam sits at the drums and Jimmy goes through the guitars. Zach sets up a mic on a stand off to the side and motions for us to join him.

"For tonight's rehearsal, we'll pretend the wall with the door is the audience," Zach tells us. "You two just stand here and sing into the mic."

I curse myself for what I'm about to say, but it can't be avoided. So much for not looking uncool.

"Sorry, Zach, I don't know all the lyrics."

He shrugs. "You're backup singers. You don't sing all the lyrics, that's why this is so perfect."

Max and I look at each other with excited grins. Maybe this won't be so bad. Zach lets out another gravelly laugh.

"Rick will tell you what to sing for 'T-R-O-U-B-L-E', but for 'Highway', I just want you to sing the words, 'highway' and 'love', during the chorus. We'll go through it once, and I'll stand right here with you to show you when to sing. Okay?"

We both nod, and I clap my hands together and jump up and down a little.

"Let's rock, Max," I say with a stupid grin, which earns me a nudge with one of his crutches.

The Rebels begin to play, which is louder than I expected in this giant house. I recognize the song as one of their greatest hits. Zach steps over and turns the mic on, singing the first verse as a solo. When we get to the chorus, all the guys join in, and Zach raises a finger every time the words "highway" and "love" are in the chorus. It takes a couple of rounds to get the hang of it, but soon Max and I are singing backup without Zach having to prompt us. The song ends, and all the Rebels applaud us.

"Well done!" Zach exclaims. "I thought I might have to shut off your mic if you two couldn't hold a tune, but you did great."

We accept all the high-fives we're given, and Rick steps forward to set us up for the Travis Tritt song he wants to sing. This chorus is a bit more complicated, but we pick it up almost as easily as "Highway to Love."

Zach shoves a stool behind Max and motions for him to sit. He adjusts the mic, so it's a little lower.

"I don't want you falling on stage, man. And that's not good for your knee."

Suddenly, Max looks at us all with an alarmed expression.

"Hey, we're supposed to be in disguise, right? She'll know it's me when she sees the crutches."

Zach shrugs again. "The *Rebels* need to be in disguise, mate. You want her to know it's you. Trust me."

I nod in agreement, and Max looks around the room at us. I'm not sure if it's The Royal Rebels or the fact that he has every guy in our rapidly growing inner circle going up to bat for him, but he relaxes.

"All right then," he tells us. "Let's keep rehearsing so we get this down pat. We've got a contest to win."

Chapter 6

Scarlet

"This is so unfair," Ashley mutters as she scowls at her canvas. "Why did I have to get stuck between you two? You're artists."

I scoff. "I am not."

Merry leans back and looks at me from Ashley's other side.

"That floor you painted in the warehouse says differently."

I smile to myself as the image comes to mind. It was beautiful. My friends and I were entering a home decor contest, and we took over a warehouse so we could each create two rooms for the judges to view. Mine had a painted floor that was some of my best work.

I look at Ashley's canvas and give her a nudge.

"There is absolutely nothing wrong with yours. It's really pretty."

She tilts her head at it. "It's too…precise. Yours is so flowy. Yours too, Merry."

I look between mine and Merry's. Merry is a different kind of artist. Her medium is usually buttercream and other types of icing. Bottom line, we're both handy with a paintbrush.

"I think it's nice," Merry says, giving Ashley a wink.

"Art is all perception, Ash," I tell her. "The artist comes out in it every time. You are a precise kind of person. This is totally you, and totally gorgeous."

Ashley's expression softens as she takes another glance at her painting. We're all painting a version of Van Gogh's Starry Night. It's a Halloween version, which is awesome. There are gnarled trees that look haunted, and the moon has spooky clouds over it. Since we're painting at a place called Artsy in the Hollow, there is also a Headless Horseman in the darkened forest. I love how this town celebrates the story that made it famous.

My clouds and stars are very soft and swirly, closer to the original. Ashley's are symmetrical and very precise. There's absolutely nothing wrong with her painting, and I think it's adorable that she's miffed at it.

"Think about how you and Marina have always kind of gravitated to each other," I tell her. "While Merry and I tend to do the same. You and Marina are precise and meticulous in many ways, while Merry and I—"

"Are a couple of hot messes," Merry chimes in.

I snort. "I'd say we're just more comfortable with mess. Abstract. That's all."

Ashley's gaze darts from her painting to mine, to Merry's, and back to her own. She smirks.

"I still think yours are better. But I guess this isn't bad."

"Not bad at all," Merry pipes in. "And I couldn't write a children's book to save my life, so you have talent I can't even touch."

I get up to stretch my legs and walk around. I'm pretty much done with mine, so I decide to be nosy and look at everyone else's. Beth's painting looks great. She decided to paint an airplane crossing the moon in shadow because she loves to travel. When I get to Marina's, I have to stifle a laugh. Very precise, just like Ashley's, but still a lovely rendition of Van Gogh's original. Bella, however, has done something

I think Van Gogh might have a problem with. Although, would he be okay with a Headless Horseman in the painting? Probably not.

Bella sits back so I can get the full view of the famous killers she's painted into the forest. The Headless Horseman is joined by Michael Myers from Halloween, Jason from Friday the 13th, that weird thing from the Saw movies, and even the shark from Jaws. She painted water in the middle for him to pop out of. There's also a sign painted in scary red letters that reads "Hella Bella's Forest".

"Wow, Bella."

She laughs maniacally. "I thought the horseman needed friends. I might have gotten a little carried away."

I shake my head. "I think it looks great. You wouldn't ever catch me walking through that forest, but I think it's awesome."

Bella laughs and gets back to work putting blood on a knife, and my mind wanders to Andrew and what he and the guys are doing. They'll be at the hockey game right now. I know he'll have fun with that.

I have such love in my heart for that man, especially after our quick chat in the cottage before we left. When he told me he was determined to support Max, who has definitely become a sort of adopted little brother to Merry, Ashley, and me...well, that got me right in the feels. Then again, everything Andrew does touches my heart in some way.

I take my seat again and grab my wine glass, sipping as I enjoy the fragments of conversations between my friends as they paint. I feel myself settling. Not in a bad way. In a very good way. Things got frantic so quickly once I received the offer to have my own TV show where I design interiors and restore community spaces around the country. Add our first home purchase and our wedding into the mix, and it's no mystery why there's been some turmoil. But now things are settling into an easier pace, and I'm happy to have this time to enjoy my friends.

"I've always wanted a destination wedding," Beth says with a sigh.

"It'll be gorgeous," Merry tells her.

"No, he won't be surprised one bit," Bella replies to Marina when asked if Sam will be surprised at the number of famous killers she's painted into her forest. "I'll go over some of this with some glow-in-the-dark paint I have at home. We love Halloween."

I take another sip of wine and laugh under my breath. Sam and Bella have the cutest relationship. The woman is hell on wheels when it comes to being their band manager, but she melts into a little pile of goo whenever she and Sam are together. So sweet.

Our painting instructor has been walking around, taking in everyone's paintings. She moves to the front of the room and clears her throat to get our attention.

"It looks like everyone is winding up and putting their final touches in," she says with a broad smile. "You have ten minutes left, and then you can leave your paintings here for now. Once they're truly dry, we'll wrap them up and deliver them to Marina's place tomorrow."

I take one final look at mine and decide it's done. I already know what I'll do with it. When we get home, I'm going to go shopping at thrift stores in search of the perfect frame. It'll need to be ornate and gothic-looking, for sure. I'll paint it black and maybe give it a little dusting of purple as well. We'll hang it when we decorate the house for Halloween every year, and it'll be the perfect reminder of this wonderful weekend with my friends.

***

An hour later, Merry gasps and grabs an orange sweater off the rack of a boutique our little group stepped into as we explored the town. She holds it up against her body and grins down at it, then up at me. It's super cute. It looks very soft, and there's an adorable black cat on the front with big green eyes. I nod in approval.

"That's adorable."

Merry clutches the sweater to her chest.

"And it's mine. I love it."

"I'm glad to see you warming up to cats," I tease.

When Andrew and I had our housewarming/surprise wedding at our house, our cat Teeny decided Merry's lap was the perfect napping spot. She was a bit freaked out at first, but I could see her softening when the purring started.

"I'll have to get used to them," she says, prompting a curious look from me. "That's how spinsterhood starts. Cats. You get one, then you decide it needs a friend. Then you have four. Before you know it, you're the crazy cat lady on the block. All alone. No husband, no kids."

I roll my eyes at her. "Stop with the spinster stuff, dude. It's sooo not true."

Merry smirks. "The big three-oh is getting closer and closer."

I laugh out loud at that one.

"It's not even your next birthday. Besides, who says being thirty and single equals spinster status? And who even uses that word anymore?"

She's undeterred.

"The Cat Distribution System will find me," she says ominously. "It's just a matter of time."

"The Cat Distribution System?"

We step over to the next rack, and I pull out a cute black blazer to look at as she nods at me.

"You know all those videos where someone's just randomly walking to their car in a parking lot and they hear a kitten crying? Or a cat just shows up at their house one day and won't leave? Or what about that guy who found all those kittens on the side of a road? That, my friend, is the Cat Distribution System at work."

"That was such a cute video," I murmur. "I'm so glad he kept them safe and found them all homes."

Merry pulls up a black sequined tube top, makes a face, and puts it right back.

"Some day it'll find me," Merry mutters as she flicks through the rack without really looking at anything. "And then my transformation will begin."

I look at my friend and stay silent. Merry is one of the kindest, most caring people I know. There is no way that she's meant to stay single, unless that is what her heart wants. But I know her heart, and that isn't what she wants. When she gets focused on a thing, though, there is no breaking that focus. We've all learned the hard way. Instead of arguing, I pull a move out of her own playbook.

"Unless you find your person," I say lightly.

Merry is the first one who told me Andrew was my person, and I didn't believe her. She narrows her gaze at me.

"I see what you're trying to do," she says coyly. "But I do have to admit that it is entirely possible I will actually meet my person."

I raise my eyebrows in surprise, making her laugh.

"I can admit things, you know. I'm not that stubborn."

Now it's my turn to laugh. "You're pretty stubborn, girl. But it's not without warrant. And you have been on some horrendous dates."

She nods her head. "Right? Who did I anger in the heavens to earn such monumentally bad dating experiences? I'm a nice person."

I grin at her. "Definitely."

"I deserve to date nice men."

"Absolutely."

"So where are they?" she asks seriously. "Are they all hiding? Am I being pranked?"

I pull Merry in for a hug, crushing the kitty cat sweater between us. I give her a good, long squeeze and let her go.

"I know it feels that way sometimes," I tell her quietly. "But please don't give up. He's out there."

Merry regards me with a mixture of sadness and hope.

"Either him or the Cat Distribution System," she says, wiggling the sweater at me. "I'm going to go pay for this."

As she walks away, I say a silent prayer that her person shows up soon. For her sake. Merry has always been the unicorn of our group. Silly, fun, joyful. Ridiculously extra. I can't handle sad Merry. I want to wring the neck of every idiot guy she's dated lately. She deserves better.

Bella steps over and gasps in delight as she plucks the black sequined tube top off the rack and adds it to the basket she's carrying. If anyone can make that look good, it's Bella. The woman has no fear.

I step outside into the cold October air and join Marina and Beth, who gave up pretty quick and came out here to sit on a bench and wait for us. Marina's expression sobers when she sees my face.

"Something wrong?"

I shake my head. "Not really. Just Merry and the spinster stuff again. I hate this for her."

"I am dying to set her up on a date, but she won't let me," Marina shares. "I don't know how to help."

I nod solemnly.

"Honestly, I think the best way to help is to just keep supporting her," I say. "And we need to make more time for girl dates. The four of us. I'll make it the highest priority."

Marina grabs my hand and squeezes. "Me too."

Ashley, Merry, and Bella come bursting out of the shop with happy smiles, toting their purchases. Beth bolts up off the bench with a grin that's almost maniacal.

"Candle shop?"

Bella laughs and shakes her head.

"Girl, how many candles do you have at home? You're obsessed. You're gonna set the house on fire."

Beth shrugs. "Can't help it. I like what I like."

We start walking toward the candle shop together, and I loop my arm through Beth's.

"It's okay," I tell her. "I know a fireman."

Beth laughs, and we walk down the sidewalk towards the candle shop with our friends. The crisp air tingles on my cheeks as we walk. Everywhere I look, the town is on fire with the colors of fall. A lot of the trees have shed their leaves, but they're on the ground, which creates a colorful path up this picturesque street lined with little shops. Some have fall or Halloween-themed wreaths on their doors. It makes me want to grab a hot cup of cider and sit in a window somewhere, watching the world go by.

A bell over the shop door jingles as Marina pulls it open, holding it for us as we all file in. The scents of cinnamon and nutmeg immediately tickle my nose as I enter. Large wooden bookcases line the walls of the shop, and there are several round wooden display tables in the center. Every size and shape of candle is on offer in this place, and I find myself feeling a little jealous that this isn't my life. Owning this charming little shop in the cutest little town, making candles, and selling them.

The idea loses a little luster when I think about winter here. The snow. The cold. I'm a native Californian. I have no idea how to survive in the snow. It sounds romantic, but I would probably make a mess of it. I'm definitely better off just visiting Zach and Marina when the mood hits me. I'll stick to San Francisco.

Merry wastes no time stepping over to a display of candles in jars, colorful labels prompting shoppers to sniff them. I look at a few and laugh. They're named things like "Smells like a day at the beach", "Smells like the best day ever", and "Smells like a new puppy". I watch as Merry picks up a tester candle and sniffs it.

She rolls her eyes and plops it in my hand, muttering, "Doesn't smell like anything like me."

I look down at the label and laugh.

Smells like a Unicorn.

***

After hours of shopping, our driver pulls up into the estate's circular driveway, and we pull ourselves out of the back in a tangle of shopping bags and tired groans. Ashley and I head for the side gate, which opens to a path that leads to the guest houses in the back, but she stops short, and I nearly run right into her.

"Hey, what—"

She holds up a hand and motions for me to listen. I don't hear anything at first, but when Marina opens the front door to the house, the sound is much louder. The sound of the guys rehearsing for tonight's karaoke contest. Ashley and I exchange excited looks and head for the front door instead. We file in behind Bella, who makes a beeline for the music room with the rest of us.

I'm not fully prepared for what I see. The Royal Rebels don't surprise me at all. Rick is on guitar, Zach is in front at the mic, and Sam is at the drums. Jimmy's on bass. No, what I'm not prepared for is Max and my sweet Andrew standing at a mic looking like rock stars in mirrored sunglasses as they sing backup. Well, Max is sort of leaning on a stool, he's not fully standing, but they look like they do this every day.

Zach makes eye contact with Marina as we walk in, and he immediately begins singing to her, which always tugs at my heartstrings. They're adorable together. We all drop our bags on the coffee table so we can applaud and cheer when they finish the song. Andrew pulls his sunglasses off, and I can't hold back. I walk straight over to him and kiss both of his beautiful dimples, and then press my lips to his. His arms wrap around my waist as teasing taunts erupt from the guys. Something about newlyweds and kissy kissy…I don't care. I have to kiss my rockstar fireman.

"You guys sound so great!" Bella says with a laugh. "Max, Andrew… any time you need representation, you just let me know."

Max laughs, and I pat him on the shoulder.

"You sound so great," I tell him. "Marina's not the only singer in the family."

"She is, as far as I'm concerned," he says. "This is a one-night-only gig for me. For Gabi."

I click my tongue and ruffle his hair. "Aww!"

"Can we hear it from the beginning?" Marina asks.

I grin at Andrew. "Oh, yes, please!"

I'm rewarded with a laugh and a wink that tells me I'll pay for that later. Not that I mind.

We all grab seats on the couches as the guys start up "Highway to Love again". I'm not sure if I'll ever get used to being on close personal terms with The Royal Rebels, one of the most famous indie rock bands today. So many fans would give an arm or a leg to watch this private concert we're getting in Zach's music room, and yet this is normal for me now. Well, it is ever since the four of us got Zach's attention when we were singing with Marina in a traffic jam. Now it's nothing for me to be visiting them in San Francisco and listening to Zach play around on his piano or with his guitar. He writes hit songs as fast as regular people do a load of laundry. And here he is rehearsing with the Rebels and my husband so they can all get his brother-in-law a date. Surreal.

They go through the song once more, and we start seriously cheering them on. We're clapping to the beat of the music, and Beth sends us all into fits of hysterical laughter when she pulls out her wallet and starts throwing one-dollar bills in the air. When they finish the song, we cheer and whistle as they bow.

"Can you guys do 'T-R-O-U-B-L-E' now?" Marina begs.

Her eyes sparkle with delight when Ashley lets out a little whimper. I laugh under my breath. Ashley loves to watch Rick perform, and he'll be up front for this one since he's doing the country song. His eyes lock with hers, and he offers her a slow grin that's so sexy I feel bad watching. I look to Andrew, who is quietly snickering at my reaction.

Rick steps up to the mic, and Zach gets behind the piano. Sam counts them off, and Rick and Jimmy let loose on their guitars. The entire room fills with the upbeat, heart-pounding melody, and we're instantly on our feet.

It is the most adorable, swoony thing to see Rick as he sings this song. He will not take his eyes off of Ashley, and if looks alone could seduce a woman, she would be a puddle of goo on the carpet right now. Wow.

Zach does a tremendous job on the piano, banging out a solo that would have the entire bar in an uproar if they were actually playing instruments tonight. This is a serious jam session, and I feel lucky to catch it. Even without instruments tonight, our whole group is just going to get out-of-control nuts, and I am here for it. This is going to be so fun.

Max and Andrew are completely on board with their backup vocals, and I am seriously impressed with my husband's hidden talent. I'm going to have to get him to do some of these little backup singer dance moves he's doing right now...later in private. I don't know how, but he manages to be drop-dead sexy and completely adorable at the same time.

As the song finishes, we burst into applause and cheers again. Andrew and Max high-five each other, and the guys seem happy with how it all went. I pick through the mess of shopping bags to find my three as Marina gets everyone's attention.

"Okay, dinner isn't for a few hours," she tells us. "So make yourselves at home and do whatever you like, and we'll see you in the library for cocktails at seven. Since the karaoke contest is at ten, the car service is coming at nine to pick us up. That'll give the guys time to check in and everything."

I waste no time making my way to Andrew and taking his hand. I smile at Max as I pull Andrew away.

"Sorry, Max, I need to steal this man away for a bit."

Max laughs softly as I drag my sweet husband out of the room and into the hall. He instantly wraps his arms around me and pulls me against him, and I melt into his embrace. He drops little kisses along my jawline, and I let out a little groan. I nudge him again, and we start walking toward the kitchen and the French doors. Once we're outside and heading across the backyard, I shift the bags in my hands and wrap an arm around his waist as we walk.

"So, that looked amazing," I tell him. "How long were you guys practicing?"

He gives me a smug sideways glance.

"It's called rehearsal, babe," he jokes. "Music industry stuff you wouldn't understand."

"Oh boy," I moan. "Now that you're a rockstar, you're going to be such a diva."

Andrew laughs and kisses the side of my head. He uses his key to unlock the cottage door, then holds it open for me. I plant a quick kiss on his lips as I pass, then head to the bedroom to drop the bags off.

I check my reflection in the bathroom mirror and decide I'm going to redo my makeup before we go to the pub tonight. And maybe change my outfit. I hear him puttering around in the little kitchenette and head back out to join him. He's just bringing out two diet sodas and two glasses of ice when we meet in the living room.

"Well, that's just what I wanted," I tell him as he sets everything down and plops onto the couch.

"I thought you might be thirsty after all that cheering."

I lean closer and wink at him. "I wasn't talking about the diet soda, hot stuff."

Without a word, he grabs me and pulls me onto his lap as I squeal for my life. I wrap my arms around his broad shoulders as he claims my lips with his own. I love his soft, sweet kisses. Kisses that make me feel like I'm the most special, treasured woman on this earth. We kiss each other for, well...I don't know how long. It doesn't matter. It's nice to be alone for a bit.

"I don't want to ruin the mood, but do you have anything resembling a bandana that I can use for tonight?"

I laugh softly against his lips.

"I think I can find something that might work," I tell him. "It might be a pastel, though. Are you okay with that?"

He presses our foreheads together and smiles.

"Baby, I'm about to go on stage with The Royal Rebels and act like I belong up there," he grumbles. "Do you think I care what color the bandana is? I just want to fit in as much as possible."

I laugh and nod. "So you guys are going for the cowboy look?"

"It makes sense," he says. "There's a costume contest right before, and all the advertising for the event says costumes are welcome. Bandanas and cowboy hats will hide those famous faces."

I gasp. "I don't have a cowboy hat for you."

"Apparently, Zach is fascinated by the American cowboy," Andrew explains. "He has enough hats for all of us. It's bandanas that are the problem."

"I think I have a purple one. If not...All I have to offer are polka dots."

Andrew grimaces adorably.

"Then I'll be the most fearsome looking polka dot-wearing cowboy Sleepy Hollow ever saw."

I melt into a smile and kiss him soundly. "I love you so much. You make everything better."

His soulful brown eyes roam over my face. "Truly?"

"One thousand percent better. Always."

"I love you, too, baby. More than anything."

***

A few hours and about two hundred kisses later, Andrew and I are seated in the beautiful green and gold formal dining room up at the main house. The entire party is seated around a beautiful, long dining table that is fully decked out. Flowers. Candles. The works. Anyone could walk in here and think the King of England was coming for dinner. Well, except for the fact that the candelabras are black and purple. They're sitting on shiny silver trays that reflect the light. Strands of silver and pearl beads are strewn lavishly around as if a pirate's horde was looted for the decorations. And the flowers are black as well, dyed roses with silver accents and gauzy purple bows. The effect is as spooky as it is breathtaking.

At the moment, Jimmy is regaling us with the story of when he met Zach and Rick and challenged them to a guitar duel in a bar during spring break. Apparently, he thought Zach and Rick were a little too cocky, and he wanted to take these two spoiled Juilliard boys down a peg or two.

"So who won?" Ashley asks.

All hands point to Jimmy, and he sits back in his chair with a smug expression.

"Who's cocky now, mate?" Zach teases.

I lean over to Andrew. "Do you want anything from the dessert table?"

He smiles and shakes his head, so I get up and dish myself a second helping of tiramisu. It's not as wonderful as Nonno's, but nothing is. This is a perfectly respectable tiramisu, however, and I am on vacation. I intend to enjoy all the things. I wander back to my seat, and Andrew plants a sweet kiss on the corner of my mouth to welcome me back.

"How are you gents feeling about tonight?" Zach asks Max and Andrew.

Andrew gives a quiet thumbs up, and Max holds up his beer. "I'm ready!"

It's weird to see him with a beer, but he turned twenty-one a few months ago. Our baby brother is growing up so fast.

All the guys are wearing jeans and boots. Some are cowboy, some are not. Some have shirts that look a little more Western than others. All of them have bandanas around their necks, which they'll pull up over their famous faces when we're in the pub. Zach explained to us that they won't mute their voices much, and the Rebels are used to projecting those voices when they're in concert.

I look over at Andrew.

"Are you really feeling okay about all this?"

His loving gaze nearly melts me to the chair.

"Yep," he tells me. "We're all in it for Max. Although I have a confession."

"Oh?"

"I'm also in it for that madly-in-love look you get on your face because I'm making a fool of myself."

I laugh softly and shake my head.

"You're not making a fool of yourself, baby," I tell him. "You know me. I'd tell you if you were terrible, I'd just be nice about it because I love you."

Andrew laughs out loud and nods. "You're right, you would."

I take a bite of my dessert and look around the table at my friends. There are about twenty different conversations going on at the same time, but no one cares. We're all having a great time. Merry clears her throat and points to her watch, catching Marina's eye. Zach checks his watch as well.

"Right," he says with a devilish grin. "It's time to go, friends. Are we ready?"

We're all ready. This is going to be some night. We all begin to stand, and Andrew pulls my chair out for me as I get up. I smile up at him.

"I can't wait to cheer you on," I tell him. "I'm so grateful for you."

The catering staff begins bustling about the back of the room as we leave, and Andrew laces our fingers together. He brings my hand up to his lips and kisses the back of it.

"Well, as Zach would say, let's go to the pub."

I steal a glance at Max, who is trying his best to hide an adorable, excited grin. I say a silent prayer that the guys are able to pull this off tonight and everything goes well. With that, the whole group heads out the front door to the awaiting car service vehicles. Everyone's bantering excitedly back and forth, and we make quick work of deciding who is riding with who. After a chorus of car doors slamming, we're off into the night and ready for The Royal Rebels and their two extra band members to steal the show. And hopefully Gabi's heart.

III

Ashley & Rick

Chapter 7

Ashley

I nestle into Rick's side in the back of the car, relishing in his warmth and the feel of the protective arm he wraps around me. I look up at him in the dark, trying to figure out what he's up to. There's a restless energy about him that isn't his usual pre-concert vibe. He catches me looking and smiles down at me, making my pulse flutter and my stomach dip in a very familiar way.

"What's up with you tonight?"

He just keeps smiling.

"I'm just happy, that's all."

I shift in my seat so I can face him more.

"No, that's not it. Are you up to something?"

As much as he tries to hide it, there's a light in his eyes I know very well. *Very*, very well. Yes, he's up to something. And now I'm grinning like an idiot because I know something's up, and he's looking at me with a stubborn expression that tells me I won't be getting any secrets out of him today. I run a finger from his hip to his knee, which is a long way because the man is tall.

"I can't wait to see you up there looking like a train robber with a bandana over your face," I tease. "Even if it's a shame to cover that perfect mug of yours."

"Don't worry about that," he says with a wiggle of his eyebrows. "I plan to seduce you with just my eyes showing, Fireball."

I laugh softly and rest my head on his shoulder as the car slows. We must be getting close to the pub. A realization creeps in as I think about the songs they're performing tonight, and the fact that Rick chose the country song they're singing. Uh oh.

"Hey, what are you up to?" I ask in a near whisper, raising my head to look at him. "Does this have to do with that Travis Tritt song?"

The song Rick chose for the guys to perform tonight, "T-R-O-U-B-L-E", is one of Rick's favorites. Nothing makes him happier than to sing it in the kitchen while we're cooking dinner, and he sings it to me as if I'm the trouble in the song. It makes me laugh, and it makes me all swoony when he starts in with the sexy dance moves.

He looks down at me with a devilish grin, and I let out a nervous laugh. It's one thing to be the focus of all his attention when we're alone, but if he's up on a stage in his element…singing that song to me…oh, help. I can see by the recognition in his eyes that he knows I've guessed where he's going with this.

Rick presses a kiss to my temple, then trails little kisses all down the side of my face before moving those lips next to my ear.

"I've got you right where I want you, Fireball."

I throw my head back and laugh as the car pulls to a stop. We're in the same car as Zach, Marina, Sam, and Bella.

"Alright, cowboys," Zach says. "Saddle up."

I grin as Rick, Zach, and Sam pull their bandanas over their faces like train robbers in the old western movies. Car doors start opening. Rick opens his door and steps out, then offers me his hand. I take it and scoot myself out until he pulls me into his arms. Those ocean blue eyes of his twinkle at me.

"Wish me luck, woman," he growls in a kind of Clint Eastwood Old West way.

I grin up at him. "Always. And I have a request, if I may."

He nods.

"Have mercy on me in there."

Rick lets out a low laugh and wraps his hand around mine.

"Not a chance."

And with that, he tugs me toward the entrance of the Headless Horseman Pub and what is sure to be an unforgettable night.

***

The inside of the pub is just freaking cool. Dark-stained wood walls and brass hardware on a huge bar that wraps around the bartender, giving it an old-world pub vibe. The bar sits on the right side of the room, and the rest of the space is taken up with wood tables and chairs. A stage suitable for live music is on the back wall, and a small platform for a DJ is right next to it. The bar is packed tonight, with many people in costume. None of the ladies in our group wore one. We just dressed up a little for a night out.

Bella zips to the front of our group, heads over to the bar like she owns the place, and flags down a staff member. There's some chatting back and forth, a handshake, and we're waved over to some reserved tables in front of the stage. The tables are slightly off to the right, but we'll have a great view of the contest from here. Two servers come in and move our tables together, and I watch in awe as Bella slips tips into each of their hands. We take our seats, and Marina gives Bella a wide-eyed grin.

"What?" Bella says with a shrug. "I hate crowds, so I called ahead and offered them a rather large tip if they'd reserve a space for us."

Marina nods appreciatively. "I'm impressed. Thank you for thinking of that."

I steal a glance toward the area by the bar where contestants were told to wait. The guys are all clustered together and keeping their heads down, even with the disguises. A smart move just in case there's a big Rebels fan back there with them. Zach's British accent is a dead giveaway.

Scarlet nudges my arm as Max breaks away from the group and carefully maneuvers himself on crutches to a table on the other end of the front row. There's a small group of people at the table where he stops, and I think I know who Gabi is, just gauging from facial expressions. There's one young woman with sunny blonde hair and pretty blue eyes who lights up when Max walks up. And she's dressed like a dalmatian. Seems like something a person who loves animals would do.

I look around at Marina, Merry, Beth, and Bella, and we're all watching Max with way too much interest. I laugh under my breath, and Marina meets my gaze. She puts her hand over her heart and makes a funny, lovesick face, and I nod. It is incredibly sweet to see Gabi's reaction to Max. There is definitely a connection there.

Max points to the guys at the back of the bar, and Gabi's face lights up again. He's obviously telling her he brought a group to compete in the contest for her charity. She bolts out of her chair and throws her arms around Max's neck.

"Oh my gosh, I'm gonna die from the cuteness," Merry says, sitting back in her chair.

"I know," Marina says. "They look so sweet together."

Max turns in our direction, and we all jump in our seats, actively looking at anything but him. I see him smirk at us out of the corner of my eye, and he heads towards us on his way back to the guys.

"Smooth, ladies," he says as he passes, and we all burst into laughter.

A server sidles up to Bella's chair with a huge smile on her face.

"Welcome, ladies, can I get you anything?"

I'm pretty sure Bella's going to be treated like royalty all night, thanks to the money she flashed to get reserved seats. Not that I mind, because we'll benefit too. We all order our drinks and some appetizers, because Beth is a bottomless pit. She gets teased for it, but she can eat like a linebacker and not gain any weight.

Merry leans forward so she doesn't have to raise her voice over the noise of the crowd, and we all lean in.

"That girl is half in love with Max already, don't you think?"

I steal another look. Gabi looks like she's having fun with her friends, but she's clearly talking to them about Max. She keeps peeking over her shoulder at him, and she's smiling like a lovesick puppy. I am sooo going to enjoy watching this story unfold tonight. I think we all are.

Bar patrons erupt into a crazy chorus of cheers and applause as a tall, thin man dressed like Jack Skellington jumps onto the stage. He grabs a wireless microphone off a mic stand and holds his arms out, welcoming the attention that he's getting. Obviously, a local who loves this bar and this town.

"Welcome, friends! I'm Pete Cassidy, your host for our boo-tiful karaoke contest tonight."

More applause, and he looks out into the crowd excitedly.

"As usual, this time of year, we have a lot of guests from out of town, and I want to say welcome to the Headless Horseman Pub!"

Even more cheers, especially from our group, since we are definitely from out of town.

"So I was just back there reviewing our list of contestants, and we have six amazing groups for your consideration this evening. They drew numbers to see who goes on in what order, and they arrrrre," he says dramatically as he pulls a piece of paper from his pocket. "The Icky Ichabods, Grandma's Boys, The Sunflowers, Rockin Regulars, Dave and Ken, and the Mad Dog Cowboys."

Polite applause this time, and Pete pulls a five-gallon bucket full of candy out from backstage to show the audience.

"Tonight's contestants will sing two songs each. Winners will be decided by our three lovely judges up here at this table front and center, but they will be taking the audience response into consideration in their final judgment. Tonight's winner gets this giant bucket of sugar and five thousand dollars donated to their charity of choice. Are we ready?"

The bar erupts into cheers and applause so loud I'm starting to worry about what my hearing will be like at the end of the night. This crowd really knows how to celebrate. Marina leans over excitedly.

"I'm guessing they're the Mad Dog Cowboys," she says. "I'm glad they're last. They're gonna have this whole bar screaming like crazy."

I nod, laughing. "This is the best. I'm having so much fun already. I can't wait for them to take the stage!"

"Before we bring out our first contestants," Pete begins as two stagehands set up three mics behind him. "How about a round of applause for our judges? Matt Stevens, Mayor of Sleepy Hollow, Cheryl Sanborn, President of our chamber of commerce, and Maya Parker, owner of this fine establishment!"

We all applaud for the judges as they stand and wave. Pete motions for a group of guys to get up on stage as he turns to address the crowd once more.

"First up, and I must say these guys are my favorites just because of their name...the Icky Ichabods singing for the Tarrytown Food Pantry!"

Everyone applauds again as three guys about our age get up on stage. They raise their arms to get the crowd going, and they all take a position at a mic.

"Uh, hey everybody," the one in the middle says. "We're gonna do '1999' by Prince first."

A smattering of applause ripples through the bar as the DJ starts the karaoke track. Their vocals aren't bad, but they're definitely not a threat to our guys. I feel bad just thinking that, since they're professional musicians - but since Zach and Marina are donating to everyone tonight, it's exciting to watch. I love that every contestant is going to win tonight.

The Icky Ichabods perform "All My Exes Live in Texas" for their country song, which kind of makes the crowd a little sleepy. Probably not what they were going for, but they get a good amount of applause and the judges hold up giant scorecards for the whole bar to see at the end of their performance. On a scale of one to ten, they get fives from two judges and a six from the third.

Next up is the group called Grandma's Boys, who turn out to be two jokesters who want their fifteen minutes of…fame? They're singing for another food pantry in the area. They're atrocious singers, but very funny - and clearly banking on their humor to get them through the night. The judges give them all threes.

Now it's the Sunflowers' turn, and they are just the cutest. Two little old ladies in matching dresses with sunflowers on them. They have big straw hats decorated with sunflowers as well. The crowd goes absolutely nuts as they take the stage. Marina and I exchange curious looks, and I know she's thinking the same thing I am. Are the Rebels about to get shut down by these two little old ladies? That'll be a story we tell for the rest of our lives.

"Our charity is Miss Kitty's Cat House Rescue, and for our rock song, we're going to do 'I Wanna Hold Your Hand' by the Beatles," one of them says, giving us a double thumbs up and a toothy smile.

Merry leans over to Scarlet and says something about cat distribution that I don't quite understand. Scarlet rolls her eyes and shakes her head emphatically.

The Sunflowers are so adorable. They have choreography, and we can barely hear them through the cheers coming from the crowd. I take a peek back at the guys and find them cheering just as loud as the rest of us. Rick finds me and quickly lifts the bandana from his face. He mouths *I love you* at me. I do it right back. Be still my heart.

Next, the Sunflowers perform "Goodbye Earl" by the Dixie Chicks, and the entire bar is on their feet by the end of it. These ladies gave it their all, and I want to start a fan club for them. They do a few adorable curtsies as the judges give them three tens. Oh, boy…the competition is fierce.

I look over at Marina to see her laughing hysterically at her phone. She holds it up for me to see a text from Zach.

Darling Siren, I might be leaving you and running away with Gladys from the Sunflowers.

I turn to look for Zach and spot him hurrying through the crowd towards Marina after she aims her best pouty lip at him. He bends over and wraps her in his arms quickly, buries a kiss on her neck, and rushes back to the guys. All without losing his cowboy hat.

The next two acts are nothing to worry about. Both are fun groups, but they don't get anywhere close to the thunderous applause the Sunflowers got. My heart rate picks up as the guys appear next to the stage, waiting for Pete to introduce them.

"All right, everyone, our last act for the night…performing for Gabi's Big Dogs Pet Sanctuary…the Mad Dog Cowboys!"

My friends and I scream our heads off as the guys take the stage. Since it's karaoke, they don't have to play instruments, so it's a little weird to see them all standing at mics together. Max takes the stage first, and Andrew pulls a stool over to their mic for him. Marina grabs me by the arm when he smiles at Gabi from up on the stage. So cute.

Zach and Sam are at the mic in the middle, and Rick and Jimmy take the one closest to us. A good decision, since Zach and Rick standing next to each other at a mic might be way too obvious. The goal is still for them to get through their performances without being discovered, even if Zach is going to come clean in the end.

I can see that Zach is making an effort to rein in his energy on stage, and I give Marina a panicked look when he steps up to speak. She just laughs.

"Watch this," she says cryptically.

"Hey, y'all," Zach says in a perfect American accent.

My eyes nearly bulge out of their sockets, and I burst out laughing. I had no idea Zach had this skill in his wheelhouse. Wow.

"We're gonna do...uh...'Highway to Love' by The Royal Rebels."

I am still laughing hysterically, but no one can hear me over the applause. When this is over, I'm going to make Zach say a million different American slang words, just to test him.

The music starts, and I get the giggles again at Sam bobbing his knee like he has no rhythm. They are really working it.

Zach doesn't hold back when he starts singing, though, and the whole bar goes nuts. Because hey, who is this guy who sounds exactly like Zach Adams from The Royal Rebels? He puts quite a bit of energy into the performance, but he uses none of his usual moves. He doesn't run all over the stage or get out into the audience. He stands at the mic and uses his hands and arms to gesture a lot, but he does a good job not tipping anyone off as to who he really is.

Rick is also very reserved, but something tells me that's going to change when it's his turn and they sing "T-R-O-U-B-L-E." Lord help me, he's taken his long blonde hair out of the usual man-bun, and it's hanging loose from under the cowboy hat. He's got more than his usual stubble going on as well. That, combined with the white button-down shirt and blue jeans that fit those long legs of his, has me weak in the knees already.

The audience clamors like crazy at the end of the song, and I feel like they're giving the Sunflowers a serious challenge. Jimmy raises his arms and challenges the crowd to get louder, and Andrew and Max join in. The crowd gets even louder.

Then Jimmy moves over to join Zach and Sam at their mic, and Rick steps forward with all his usual confidence, like he's going to shut it down and put their win in the bag. Even with a bandana over that handsome face, he looks beautiful up there, and I can't take my eyes off him. He pulls the wireless mic off the stand and takes another step forward.

"Our country song is 'T-R-O-U-B-L-E' by Travis Tritt," Rick says as the audience applauds excitedly.

The music starts, and now it's Rick's turn to hold nothing back. He dances all over that stage, and the audience is so loud I can barely hear when he starts singing. He begins the first verse, and everyone starts clapping to the beat of the music.

When he gets to the chorus, he points right at me, and my heart rate goes off the charts. He sings to me, and the entire bar is clapping along and looking from me to him and back again. I feel a blush crawling up my face. There is a six-foot-four-inch Viking god on stage, and he's turned all his sex appeal on me. Marina grabs my arm as I cup my hand over my face.

Rick turns his attention to the two female judges for the next part of the song and the second chorus. I can't see their faces because they're slightly in front of us, but I can imagine they're eating it up.

Andrew and Max are doing an incredible job at their mic, and Gabi isn't taking her eyes off of him. Her friends are cheering loudly, trying to make sure the guys get proper credit for the audience response.

I am not ready for what happens next.

During the final chorus, Rick leaps off the stage and stalks towards me as he sings. Be. Still. My. Heart. This man is larger than life, and he's all mine. As he belts out the last line of the song, he pulls me up out of my seat, wraps me in his arms, and twirls me around. I squeal until he stops spinning me, then he carefully sets me back in my seat and jumps back on the stage.

The crowd doesn't calm down for what feels like ages. They're on their feet. Hats are thrown onto the stage. Someone is yelling out rapid-fire yeehaws. The energy in this bar is absolutely insane.

The judges hold up their score cards, and it's all tens across the board. A tie.

Pete jumps back up on the stage.

"For the first time ever, we have a tie!"

The audience cheers as the judges huddle together, discussing how they're going to handle this. Zach steps over and taps Pete on the back of the arm. Pete turns and gets pulled into a huddle with Rick, Jimmy, and Sam. I can see Zach pull his bandana down, and Pete steps back, laughing loudly.

"Shut up!" he says loud enough for the mic to pick it up, and then he starts laughing again.

There's now a hurried discussion happening on stage, but Pete looks excited - not angry or upset - so that's definitely good. I see Zach grinning and nodding at him as he pulls the bandana back over his face. They break up their huddle, and Pete steps forward again.

"Judges, don't worry about the tie breaker," Pete says excitedly. "I have some excellent news to share."

Gabi exchanges concerned looks with her friends until she looks at Max, who is giving her a thumbs-up signal to tell her it's going to be okay. She looks like her curiosity is going to eat her alive.

Pete grins out at the audience.

"Don't you guys think the Mad Dog Cowboys did a great job singing like The Royal Rebels?"

The audience cheers again.

Pete laughs into the mic and steps back, sweeping a hand toward the guys.

"Here's why!"

Zach, Rick, Jimmy, and Sam all take their hats off and pull their bandanas down in one perfectly synchronized move…and the entire bar goes absolutely feral. Even the judges are standing and cheering as they smile and wave at the crowd. Finally, Zach steps forward with a mic and motions for the crowd to be quiet.

"What did you think of my American accent, friends?" he growls into the mic.

The explosive applause is deafening, and Marina squeals as the judges hold up three tens for his accent. Zach laughs and takes a bow, then makes his way over to Max.

"So we just want to say thank you for letting us crash your karaoke contest," Zach says.

He wraps an arm around Max's shoulder, and Max grins over at him.

"This is my brother-in-law, Max," Zach says, prompting applause again. "Max can be a pretty persuasive guy, and he wanted to do his part to support Gabi's rescue and get it off the ground."

Gabi's expression is priceless. She looks like she's having an out-of-body experience as she watches one of the world's biggest rock stars talk about her and her dog rescue.

"It's nice to meet you, Gabi," Zach says with his trademark grin.

Gabi shakes her head in dismay, giggling like a schoolgirl. She looks at Max and mouths, *Wow*.

"We realize, of course, that it's not very cool for us to crash your charity karaoke contest and run away with the prize," Zach continues. "We're here to fight for Gabi's rescue, but all the charities represented tonight are absolutely worthy of the five-thousand-dollar prize."

More applause from the crowd.

"We told Pete the tie breaker wouldn't be necessary for two reasons. First, because we were pretty sure we were about to get beaten by the Sunflowers."

Cheers and laughter bubble up from the audience.

"And second, because we're donating five thousand dollars to all the charities tonight."

Aaaand we're back to feral. The noise level goes through the roof. Gabi screams and claps her hands over her cheeks, completely overwhelmed in the best way possible. Her dream project just became a reality. Her friends surround her, giving hugs and handing over cocktail napkins for her to dab away happy tears. Max watches from the stage with the sweetest, most lovesick grin.

Pete steps forward again and almost has to yell into the mic to be heard over the noise.

"I don't think we'll ever top this tonight, but everyone is literally a winner! Can we get all of our contestants on the stage, please? We need pictures, or I'm never going to believe this actually happened."

There's a light touch on my arm, and Marina nods at the stage with a happy grin on her face.

"Look."

I follow her gaze. Gabi leaves her friends and joins Max on the stage. He stands at the edge of it, reaching out a hand for her, and she takes it. Merry and Scarlet turn their eyes in the same direction, wondering what we're looking at. Gabi steps right up to Max and wraps her arms around him for a hug.

We have to keep ducking our heads and moving around to see, but she lets go and apparently wants him to sit back down, so he doesn't stress his knee. He listens, which makes me laugh under my breath because he never listens to Marina when she wants him to do the very same thing.

The Sunflowers toddle past us on their way to the stage, and Pete gets all the performers together for pictures. Gabi tries to get out of the shot, but Max takes her hand and shakes his head...urging her to come with him. She does, and Marina lets out a little squeal over the fact that Max doesn't let go of Gabi's hand, and she doesn't seem to want it back.

I keep glancing back and forth between Max and Gabi and the rest of the stage. One of the Sunflowers is flirting with Zach, and the Icky Ichabods are enthralled while talking with Sam and Jimmy. Andrew has managed to find his way off the stage and is pulling Scarlet into his arms. And Rick? My sweet, romantic fiancé grabs another stool from somewhere and discreetly slides it over for Gabi and then retreats.

She sits, still holding Max's hand, and the two of them carry on their conversation like they're the only two people on the planet. I feel a huge, stupid grin spreading on my face as I watch them. I know that feeling. I have it every time I'm in the room with Rick. How wonderful to watch the beginnings of it happening for Max.

Chapter 8

Rick

I think this might be the fiftieth picture I've taken with the Sunflowers. First, they had to sit in my lap. Then it was Zach's lap. After that, one on each lap, and then they switched. One of them had the other snap a photo as she kissed me on the cheek. If they weren't about eighty years old and completely adorable, I'd feel like a piece of meat right about now. Actually, I kind of still do. But it's okay. I know they're just having fun, and they're as sweet as they are funny.

I make eye contact with Ashley across the floor, and she gives me a sympathetic smile. Some days, I still can't believe she's mine. I want her in my arms right now. I've been trying to get off this stage for what feels like hours, but of course, we've caused quite a sensation tonight, and everyone wants to meet The Royal Rebels. We are definitely going to be here when the place shuts down at two am.

We're used to this. There have been plenty of times that we've decided to surprise fans in some way. It's my favorite way to engage with our fans, but tonight wasn't about that. Tonight was about Max, and rightfully so. He's an extension of Marina, whom we all fell madly in love with right around the time she fell in love with Zach. He's a pretty serious guy, mostly focused on his college studies and volunteer activities. I think the injury has shaken him a bit, and I love that our whole group just automatically jumped in to support him.

I look across the stage and find him, and I laugh under my breath. He and Gabi are seated together at one end of the stage, deep in their own little bubble. She's talking, and from the look on her face, she's expressing a lot of gratitude and amazement over what happened tonight. He looks perfectly content to just sit there in her company and listen to what she has to say. I get it. I really do.

The opening strains of Monster Mash start playing, thanks to the DJ. Gladys comes over to me in all her sunflower finery and taps me on the arm.

"May I have this dance?"

I catch Ashley grinning in the distance as I smile down at my suitor.

"I thought you'd never ask, Gladys."

She snickers, and I open my arms so we can begin a waltz. I figure a slow one is fine, and she follows my lead just perfectly. I look over the top of her head to find that Mary, the other half of the Sunflowers, has claimed Zach. When the song is over, Mary grabs Zach by the hand and leads him over to join us.

"Boys, I'm afraid it's way past our bedtime," Mary tells us. "As it is, I feel like I'll sleep for two days."

"You will!" Gladys pipes in.

Pete steps into our little group with that five-gallon bucket of candy.

"Since we never declared a winner, do you guys want to split this? It was a tie, after all."

Gladys gasps and takes off somewhere without a word to us. I laugh and shake my head. Mary plucks a small bag of M&M's from the bucket.

"This will be my treat for tomorrow," she says. "I don't want any more than that."

Zach looks between me and Mary. "Shall we just share it tonight? Let everyone take some."

"Wait a minute!" Gladys exclaims, toddling back to us with her handbag.

She starts picking through the bucket as Zach, Pete, and I look on in amusement. Mary clicks her tongue.

"Here we go," she says with an eye roll.

"Hush," Gladys snaps. "I only want a few."

Once we realize she's only taking the Butterfingers, Zach and I step in to help her find them. By the time we're done, she has about thirty of them in her bag. Pete heads off to dump piles of candy on each table in the bar.

"How are you ladies getting home at this late hour?" Zach asks them.

Mary giggles and places a dainty hand on Zach's arm.

"You're such a sweetie. My great-grandson is one of the Icky Ichabods," she shares. "He's taking us home."

"Well, it was lovely to meet you, Gladys and Mary," Zach continues. "I feel confident you would have beaten us soundly in the tiebreaker."

Gladys chuffs. "I think you would have won, but it's so nice of you to say so."

Mary pulls up double fists and gives us a tough guy face.

"We would have kicked your butts," she says, then immediately bursts out laughing with the rest of us.

We hug the Sunflowers goodbye and help them down the steps off the stage. I'm closer to my girl now, but I'm still thwarted by eager fans who just want five minutes and a quick selfie. They're everywhere. The thing is...we love our fans. I love our fans. But there's no one I love more than Ashley. I feel like I could do another four hours of this if I could just get five minutes with her. I can feel myself getting to my people threshold.

As if she's read my thoughts, Ashley ends whatever conversation she's having with Marina and comes to my side. Her arm slides around my waist, and I relax as soon as I feel her warmth against my side. One of the guys from Grandma's Boys pauses for a moment, and I introduce her. She smooths her hand down the center of my back, and I pull her in tighter, just happy that she's here.

After another hour of this, there's a lull, and Bella swoops in to share the social media buzz we created. The stories being shared from tonight are all good, our appearance was received well, and the donation to all the contestants' charities was obviously a huge hit with everyone. Bella's very happy, and that's always a good thing when it comes to the band.

Our entire group spends another thirty minutes inching our way closer to the exit. Eventually, everyone is happy with their selfies and the fact that we hung around to spend time with them. They were good sports about us crashing their contest, and tonight has been a blast.

"The cars are outside, friends," Zach says to us all. "But the men will be in one car and the ladies in another."

I laugh under my breath. Zach and I are like brothers. I know what he wants. He slaps a hand on Max's shoulder, basically confirming my suspicions. Max says goodnight to Gabi, who leaves with her friends, and the rest of us head out the door to the awaiting cars.

I give Ashley a light kiss as she steps away to join the ladies in the first car, then the guys and I all head to our own vehicle. We all get in and buckle up, and the car is barely moving before Zach turns to Max.

"Okay, spill it," he says with a wide grin. "It looks like it went well with Gabi, but we want the play-by-play."

Max, who is normally pretty straightforward, decides this is the perfect time to mess with us a little. He looks at each of us with a serious expression, pressing his lips together. The car grows silent as we wait for him to speak. Finally, he breaks into a huge grin.

"I've got a date for the Halloween party."

We all burst into cheers. Zach pulls Max into a hug and ruffles his hair. We're giving Max all the love right now. High-fives, knee slaps, nudges, you name it.

"She never really stopped getting emotional about what we did tonight," he says with pride shining in his eyes. "Every time she'd start trying to put her feelings into words, the happy tears would come. So I just want to say thank you to each of you for helping me. For helping Gabi."

Zach smacks Max on the knee. "Any time, kid."

He holds his phone up for us to see. "I got her number."

Sam laughs. "I should hope so after all this!"

"I had planned to go back home on Sunday," Max shares, looking at Zach. "But now…"

"You can stay for as long as you'd like, little brother," Zach says easily.

Max nods. "Thanks. I do have to get back to school, but I want to help her get started with the rescue. Another day or two won't hurt me."

Jimmy points to Max's knee. "You're not going to do anything crazy, are you?"

He laughs. "No, but I'm sure there's something I can do that doesn't involve carrying food bags and stuff like that."

"Assistant to the CEO," I joke, prompting another laugh.

"*Special* Assistant to the CEO," Zach adds.

"Chief Kissing Officer?" Andrew chimes in.

I roll my eyes. "Okay, let's give him a break."

Andrew laughs and looks over at Max. "Sorry, Max. Couldn't help myself."

We spend the rest of the car ride talking about the night we just had, and Zach and I get a lot of teasing over the Sunflowers and all their flirting. Mary and Gladys were funny and sweet. I really think they would have beaten us in a tiebreaker. Who votes against little old ladies? They even had *my* vote.

***

"It's beautiful out this morning," Ashley sighs as we walk together. "This was such a good idea."

I smile as we walk through the neighborhood, our fingers loosely laced together. It's cold out, of course, but we're bundled up enough. She tends to forget her coat, but I never let her. New York cold is different, though. I doubt even Ashley would forget a coat once she stepped outside.

The neighborhood is beautiful, with most of the homes on large expanses of land and surrounded by elegant wrought iron fences and gates. Many are made of old stone or brick with neatly manicured landscaping and an ample number of trees, giving a feeling of seclusion.

"I love that gothic-looking one across the street, but I could never live in something like that," Ashley tells me. "I'd feel like I was living in a movie set."

I glance at the one she's talking about, and she's right. It looks like something out of a horror film.

The sidewalk winds gently to the left, then flows slightly downhill as we continue. It's just after noon, and the sun is trying to warm us up through the chill air. Everyone slept late, since we didn't get in until after two am. We started trickling in for brunch, and then spent the rest of the morning talking about our night in the pub.

"What's this?" Ashley says as we near another estate.

The iron gates are padlocked with a chain, and there's a realtor's FOR SALE sign posted. We both step up to the gates and peer across the slightly overgrown lawn at the house. It's another beautiful house, but not made of stone like so many in this neighborhood. It looks very colonial, with white wood siding and a large wrap-around porch. The long, curved driveway that leads up to the house from the gate is lined with trees.

"Wow. In all the times I've visited Zach, I don't think I've ever seen a for sale sign in this neighborhood."

Ashley points at the house.

"Look at that gorgeous wrap-around porch," she says. "Can't you just see it all decorated with pumpkins and garlands for fall?"

I grin and place a gentle kiss on her temple. My Fireball.

"It's a great house," I murmur against her hair.

"There must not be anyone living in it. The lawn needs to be mowed," she speculates, craning her neck to read the sign. "Fourteen Autumn Lane. How charming."

"I guess kids on Autumn Lane don't need to go door to door and ask to mow lawns for money," I joke.

Ashley beams up at me. "Is that how you earned money as a kid?"

I nod. "With a single mom, my allowance wasn't very much. I mowed lawns and washed cars, mostly in the summer."

"I had a lemonade stand," she says, letting out a soft laugh. "My dad wanted me to be a businesswoman. He was trying to start me off early."

I reach out and smooth a hand down her beautiful, long hair. Ashley's father is very wealthy, but his career in finance didn't rub off on his elementary school teacher of a daughter. They're very close, though. He's a great guy, and since I grew up without a father, it's been an unexpected blessing to have him in my life.

"I can't believe your dad hasn't shown me pictures of that yet," I tease her.

She nods. "Oh, there are pictures. I'm sure he'll find them."

I laugh and pull her against me, wrapping her in my arms and holding her tight. The love I feel for this woman is unlike anything I've ever felt for anyone else. I just want to make everything perfect for her.

"It's too bad we'll miss the open house the realtor is having next week," she says, pointing to the wording on the sign. "It'd be fun to see the inside."

I give her an extra squeeze.

"You know there's this thing called the telephone," I say lightly. "You can use it to call realtors and schedule a time to look inside a house."

She laughs and steps back, pulling me away from the gate and down the sidewalk.

"I know, I know," she says. "I would never waste someone's time like that, though, just because I was curious. There might be pictures online, though. I'll look later."

As she pulls me farther away, I whip my cell phone from my pocket and sneak a picture of the realtor's sign. It might be fun to see inside this place if we can.

"So what's the plan for today again?"

Ashley loops an arm through mine.

"We're all on our own until dinner at the house," she says. "We can do whatever we want. Did you have something in mind?"

I shoot her a mischievous grin, and she swats at me.

"I wonder how Max is doing with Gabi," I tell her. "Last night couldn't have gone better."

Ashley nods. "And I love that her attention was focused on him, even after the whole bar went nuts over The Royal Rebels being there. She was just as surprised as everyone else, but she didn't gush all over you guys. She was only interested in Max."

I didn't even think about that, but she's right. It would have been a real bummer if Gabi had been more interested in meeting the Rebels than hanging with Max. We did meet her, though, and she seemed genuinely nice. Plus, she couldn't take her eyes off Max.

"Well, since we don't have to be around other people until dinner," I murmur, gently tugging her back toward Zach's. "Let's get you back to the cottage so I can focus all my attention on you."

I'm rewarded with Ashley's lyrical laughter. I lace our fingers together as we walk, enjoying the scenery. The curved street is lined with trees that are ablaze with the colors of fall. Some are bare already, but most of them have a good amount of gold, orange, and red leaves still clinging to their branches.

"I'm glad we're not out here in the dark," Ashley says quietly.

"Why's that?"

"My imagination would get away from me too quickly," she replies. "I can just imagine a Headless Horseman coming down this road, looking for his next victim."

I grin and pull her against me, burying my face in her neck.

"That doesn't scare me. I lost my head over you ages ago."

Ashley laughs musically, clinging to me, and I bring our lips together in a series of soft, slow kisses that show her exactly how much I love her.

***

Later in the day, with a plan firmly in place, I nudge Ashley with my foot and shoot her a mischievous grin. Her beautiful blue eyes flick to mine, and a soft, slow smile spreads on her face.

"What?"

We're both stretched out on the couch in the small living room at the cottage, facing each other. She shuts her laptop and sets it on the coffee table.

"Well? What's up with you?"

"You shut your laptop," I point out. "Taking a break?"

She nods. "I've done enough for now, and I'm ahead of schedule."

"Perfect timing."

She huffs. "For what? Are you going to tell me?"

I stand up and offer her my hand.

"Better. I'm going to show you. Let's go, Fireball."

Within minutes, I have her bundled up again, and we're driving away from the estate. I texted Zach earlier to ask if I could borrow his car, and I went up to the house to get the keys from him. Ashley watches me from the passenger seat.

"I love you so much," she says quietly. "I don't know what you have planned, but I love how thoughtful you are. I love that you're always thinking of things for us to do."

"I love you too, baby."

I slow the car down not far from Zach's estate, and Ashley's face lights up in surprise. We're back at the house we saw, and this time the gates are unlocked and open. I pull the car up the long, winding driveway.

"Rick!"

I grin at her as I park next to the realtor's car. She's waiting on the porch for us, smiling and waving. I look over at Ashley.

"Yes, dear?"

"You are crazy," she says, laughing. "You shouldn't have put her through all this trouble."

I smirk at my girl.

"This is literally her job," I reply. "She loves talking to people who are interested in houses."

I get out of the car without waiting for Ashley to object, walk around to her side, and open the door for her. She gets out and smiles politely at the realtor, who is still on the porch and waiting patiently.

"But we're not *really* interested in buying this house, baby. I hate wasting her time."

I raise my eyebrows at her. "How do we know whether we're interested until we see inside?"

She blinks, then her mouth drops open in surprise.

"*Are* we interested in this house?"

I mimic her expression, and she laughs.

"Maybe? Let's go look at it, Fireball."

She takes my hand and we climb the few steps up to the porch.

"Mr. and Mrs. Archer?" the realtor greets us. "It's so nice to meet you. I'm Peggy Vincent."

"Nice to meet you, too, Peggy," I reply before Ashley has a chance to correct her.

She'll be Mrs. Archer soon. And I love the sound of that.

"Come on in, this house is really beautiful."

Peggy opens the door for us, and we step into a grand entryway that must have been spectacular when it was new. There's fresh paint throughout, but the wood stain on the molding is dated. So is the tile we're standing on. I look down at Ashley with a secret smile.

"Lead the way, Mrs. Archer."

Her eyes sparkle as she smiles at me and squeezes my hand. Just that smile alone is worth this whole trip.

Ashley leads us into the living room first. It has a gorgeous stone fireplace that looks like it's out of a movie. Large windows along the back wall overlook the spacious backyard, which includes a pool. I'm sold already.

Next, we move to the kitchen. This definitely needs upgrading. The appliances are top of the line, but they're at least ten years old. The countertops and cabinets need replacing as well. It has a good footprint, but I'd replace everything in here.

"There are six bedrooms, plus the master suite," Peggy explains as we walk through the dining room and into the hall. "And then there's the cottage, of course."

"Cottage?" Ashley asks as we pause in the hall.

Peggy nods. "There's a full cottage in the back, on the other side of the pool. Two rooms, full kitchen. A lot of the homes in this neighborhood have a guest house of sorts. This one is nicer than most of them."

"Wow," Ashley murmurs as she follows Peggy down the hall.

We walk through all the bedrooms, which are nicely sized. The master suite is huge, which I love since I'm tall and like my space. All the bathrooms need upgrading. I suppress a laugh as I realize I'm mentally renovating this house already.

Ashley keeps giving me guilty looks, and I just smile at her. She forgets that I have more money than I'll ever need in life, thanks to The Royal Rebels. When we have our farewell tour and all of that is behind us, I won't ever have to work again if I don't want to. That's not going to happen, because I hate to be bored, but I'm lucky because I can do whatever I want.

"Well, thanks for showing us the house," Ashley tells Peggy, prompting a frown from both of us.

"Don't you want to see the backyard and the cottage?" Peggy says. I like her a lot.

"We don't want to be any trouble."

"It's no trouble," Peggy insists. "Are you sure?"

Before she can reply, I put my hands on Ashley's shoulders and turn her to face me.

"Do you remember when we went to Las Vegas for the weekend?" I ask her.

"Yes."

I nod. "And we rented a car and drove around the desert, too? Remember that souvenir stand out in the middle of nowhere with the UFO out in front?"

Ashley smirks. "Yes..."

"And you wanted one of those silly aliens in a mason jar. Remember?" She laughs. "Sure do."

"You didn't get it, even though I wanted to buy it for you."

She nods. "Okay, okay."

Peggy is watching us with a grin, and Ashley turns to her.

"I still talk about how I should have gotten that stupid alien in a jar."

"Right," I say, giving her a quick kiss. "Don't let the cottage become your alien in a jar, baby. Let's go see it while we have the chance."

Peggy laughs softly. "You two are so cute. Let's go."

She leads us out a set of French doors to a wide deck that needs staining. The wood looks great, though. It just needs a little love. There's a small outdoor kitchen here, and we follow Peggy down the steps to the pool level.

The pool needs upgrading as well. The landscaping looks better out here than in the front, and we follow a flagstone path to a nice-sized cottage covered in the same white siding as the main house. Peggy opens the door, and we follow her inside.

So this is where they spent all their upgrade money, I think to myself. This cottage is beautiful. The kitchen is modern, and the floors are beautiful. Peggy notices my appreciative glances.

"The homeowner was an elderly woman who felt the main house was too much for her," she explains. "She lived here in this cottage for a few years before she passed, and her children took turns living in the main house and watching over her. Since none of them wanted to keep the house, they never upgraded it - but they spared no expense keeping the cottage updated so their mother could have every comfort."

"That's so sweet," Ashley murmurs as she walks around the living room area. "I can't believe none of them wanted this house. It's so great."

Peggy nods. "I think they all preferred to have their own homes and create new memories, but I agree. I would want to stay here. This is a great house."

Ashley nods and moves down the small hallway to see the bedrooms. There's one bedroom with an en suite bathroom, and another bedroom that's by itself. There's even a half bath tucked away.

We walk back to the house while listening to Peggy talk about the pool and the storage shed I didn't see right away. We enter the main house again and head for the door. Ashley pauses in the living room and stares into the kitchen quietly. I watch her carefully. She's picturing herself in that kitchen. I can see it in her beautiful eyes. She takes one last look around, as if saying goodbye to a friend.

"Thank you so much, Peggy," she says sweetly. "We appreciate your time very much."

Peggy smiles and pulls a business card case out. She hands a card to each of us.

"It's been my pleasure," she says. "Please reach out if you have any questions or need anything at all."

We thank her and follow her out onto the porch so she can lock up. We get in the car once we've said goodbye to Peggy, and Ashley is still staring at the house.

"That porch is great, isn't it?" I prompt her.

She nods. "It is. It's perfect. Maybe we'll see it all decorated for fall next year when a new family moves in."

I grin as I turn the car around in the circular driveway.

"Yep. Maybe we will."

Chapter 9

Ashley

I plop back onto the sofa in Marina's living room after grabbing a couple of bottles of soda for the two of us from the fridge. I left Rick back at the cottage when he said he had some things to do before coming up to the house, so Marina and I are having a rare quiet moment just the two of us. Sam and Bella are out jogging, Jimmy and Beth went to Tarrytown for something, and everyone else isn't down yet, except Max, who is off helping Gabi with her rescue start-up.

"Hey," I whisper to Marina. "Remember when you freaked out because you could never be a duchess?"

Marina laughs. "Not my finest moment, but yes."

I gesture around at this beautifully decorated home.

"I think you're going to be a great duchess."

Marina takes a bow just as Merry hits the bottom of the stairs. Her eyes get huge when she sees we're the only two down here, and she runs over at full speed and dives on top of us on the couch. I grunt and push her leg off of me with a laugh.

Merry sits up and bounces on the couch. "Girl talk! We just need Scarlet."

Marina grins. "Hopefully she'll be here soon."

"So we have dinner tonight and then what?" Merry asks. "Kinda hard to top last night, right?"

"It was pretty perfect," Marina says with a sigh. "To see my baby brother and sweet little Gabi so wrapped up in their conversation. She didn't care about anyone else in that whole pub."

"You guys did a good thing last night," Merry tells her. "Giving all that money to everyone's charities was amazing. I can't believe you ever wanted to ghost that man."

"Well, I didn't want to ghost him, I just…" Marina's voice trails off as she tries to figure out how to describe the fact that she didn't want to have anything to do with Zach when she first met him. "Actually, I guess I did want to ghost him."

We all laugh, and I hear the French doors rattle in the kitchen. Just as I'm wondering if it's Rick, Scarlet comes around the corner and sees the three of us. She jumps up and down a few times, and we motion for her to get over to us.

"Girl time!" she declares excitedly.

I can't remember when it was just the four of us alone together. It's been a while. Scarlet leans over and nudges Merry.

"I started jogging."

Merry looks at her like she's grown a second head. "Yeah?"

"Yeah. Wanna go with me tomorrow? It'll be fun."

"Fun? Running on purpose is fun?"

Scarlet smirks. "It's healthy."

Merry smirks back. "Healthy doesn't necessarily mean fun. Cookies are fun. Broccoli…not so fun."

"I like broccoli," I interject.

They all smirk at me. "Of course you do," Merry says.

Scarlet heaves a huge sigh. "I've missed this so much. You guys rock."

"How's the TV show going?" Marina asks.

"Pretty well now," Scarlet replies. "I'm getting into a rhythm with it. Location shooting can be a challenge because I miss Andrew, but he's able to come to me most weekends, or the show lets me go back home for a few days. If they renew the show for a second season, I'll have more control over the schedule."

"When will you find out about that?" I ask her.

"We were supposed to find out last week, but there's been no word," she says, then shrugs. "I guess that's show biz."

"Well, I hope you hear soon," I tell her. "It's probably not awesome having that hanging over your head."

Her show is so great. They send her to different community spaces across the country that are old and tired, and she redecorates and brings them back to life.

"How's Livvie doing?" Merry asks Marina.

We all look at Marina expectantly. It's the way Merry asks, like there's been some kind of news that the rest of us weren't privy to.

"Yeah, so apparently she's being bullied by some kids at school," Marina shares. "Zach and I are trying to help her, but being all the way on the other side of the country isn't the best."

"What about her foster mom?" Scarlet asks.

Marina nods. "She's very nice and is so great at providing stability, but she only fosters. She doesn't want to adopt, so Livvie knows this isn't permanent. It's a scary situation for a kid."

Ashley looks down at her hands. "Poor kid."

"I'm sure it'll work out," Marina says, trying to stay upbeat. "Distract me with something fun. Where did you go earlier? Zach said Rick borrowed his car."

All eyes turn to me. I laugh awkwardly and wave them off.

"Rick was just being sweet," I say lightly. "We went for a walk earlier, and we saw this house for sale. I wondered what the inside looked like, and he actually called the realtor and had her come and show it. I feel a little guilty."

Merry frowns. "Why?"

"Because it was a waste of her time," I explain. "It's not like we're going to buy the house."

"Oh my gosh," Marina exclaims. "Wouldn't that be great if you guys bought it? We'd be neighbors!"

Ashley scoffs. "It's a five-million-dollar house."

Scarlet leans over and tugs at my sleeve.

"You do realize that you're engaged to a rockstar? He can buy twenty of those houses."

Marina laughs. "More than that, actually."

I shrug them off.

"I never think of that stuff. It's not why I'm marrying Rick, and I don't want him to think I'm after his money."

Now it's Merry's turn to laugh.

"He wouldn't. Your dad is super loaded. You don't need Rick's money."

I tilt my head. She has a point. Still, I'm not going to start buying houses and spending Rick's money.

"Change of subject," I declare adamantly. "Merry, what's the dating scene like?"

Uh-oh. She shoots me a withering look.

"I'm taking a break."

"Oh, no," Scarlet pipes in. "That bad? Why are guys like this?"

Merry shrugs in resignation.

"I think you guys got all the good ones. There's nothing left out there."

Marina clicks her tongue.

"I'm sure that's not true," she says, squeezing Merry's hand.

"Maybe it's time to come out of your dating hiatus," Scarlet suggests. "You can't find your person if you're not even dating."

Merry shakes her head at us. "Maybe I'm just supposed to be single."

I nod encouragingly. "If that's what you actually want, then we want that for you. But I don't think it is."

She throws herself backwards against the couch cushions with an exasperated sigh.

"It isn't," she agrees. "You're right."

We all grow silent, unsure of what to say or how to help her without repeating what's already been said. You can do this. You deserve to be happy. He's out there. Somewhere. Merry looks down at her hands and then up at all of us.

"I'm not sure he exists," she says quietly.

"He does," Scarlet says.

Merry looks at her curiously.

Scarlet nods. "He does. He's out there. Because I don't believe you'd have these feelings if he weren't. If you were meant to be alone, then your heart would be content with that."

Merry smiles softly, nodding.

"You have an enormous heart, Merry," Scarlet adds. "You are full of love and rainbows, my unicorn friend. He's out there, and you'll find him. But you're going to have to get back out there again."

She sighs again.

"Well, there's only one thing to do," Marina says.

We all look at her expectantly.

"Shopping after dinner?" she suggests with a grin. "Maybe dessert at the pie shop?"

Merry's whole face lights up, and I let out a laugh.

"That sounds good to me."

"Did someone say pie?" Bella asks as she enters the room.

Marina grins at her. "Only if you eat all your dinner, young lady."

Bella laughs. "Not a problem."

The front door opens and closes, and Max comes in with the biggest smile on his face. He heads over to Marina, kisses her cheek, and sits in the chair next to hers.

"Hey, sis," he says lightly.

Marina's smile shines brightly as she watches her brother expectantly. We all do. He looks around at each of us.

"What?"

Merry throws her hands up. "Update, dude! How are things with Gabi?"

Max sinks back against the chair with a sigh. "She's so great."

"And you're bringing her to the party tomorrow night?" I ask excitedly. "We'll get a chance to really meet her and chat?"

Max's expression sobers in the most adorable way, like he's suddenly realized he's bringing the girl he's crazy about into the clutches of his big sister and his three honorary aunties.

"What are you guys planning?" he asks suspiciously.

Marina scoffs. "Nothing. Unless you want us to."

Merry nods. "Yeah, I mean…if you're expecting it, we'll feel oblig-"

He holds his hands up quickly. "No, no. No expectations. Other than, I'd like you guys to be very, very nice."

I can't take it anymore. Max is too sweet to mess with.

"Max, we already adore her," I tell him. "She couldn't take her eyes off you all night. You'd have a reason to worry if she was instantly starstruck by The Royal Rebels, but she only had eyes for you."

He grins so widely, I feel like his face might crack. All the joy in his heart is on his face right now.

"Yeah, well. Same."

"I love this so much for you," Marina says, watching him fondly. "You deserve it."

Max clears his throat. "Okay, that's as much attention as I'm comfortable with. When's dinner?"

Marina grins and checks her watch. "An hour. Can we talk about you until then?"

Everyone laughs, and we're joined by Jimmy and Beth coming down the stairs. They sit on the couch opposite ours. Small talk ensues, but I'm only half listening. My mind drifts back to that beautiful house on Autumn Lane with the wrap-around porch. How much more perfect can you get? Autumn Lane in Sleepy Hollow.

The interior needs so much updating, but, as Scarlet would say, it's got good bones. The natural wood needs re-staining. The carpet needs to be removed and new floors put in. Wow. Listen to me acting like this house is mine. Get a grip, Ash.

"Dinner is very casual tonight, guys," Marina says. "We're having a taco night, and then if anyone would like to go back into town and keep exploring, we'll do that. Everything comes to life on Main Street after dark, and you haven't seen that yet."

"There's a guy dressed up like the Headless Horseman who rides a horse around town," Max shares, which definitely gets Bella's interest.

"Maybe you can show him your painting," Sam murmurs to her, making her laugh.

"Tacos sound perfect," I tell Marina. "Do we have margarita mix?"

Marina laughs out loud and nods. "Absolutely."

Something touches my shoulder, and I look behind me to find my gorgeous Viking god fiancé smiling down at me. I scooch over closer to Marina and pull him onto the couch beside me. He laughs under his breath and pulls me against his side. Heaven.

"What took you so long?" I murmur to him as the others keep chatting among themselves. "Is there something going on?"

"No, baby," he says sweetly. "I just needed to make a few phone calls. No big deal."

I give him a quick kiss and settle against his side again.

"So what's everyone coming to the party as tomorrow night?" Scarlet asks. "Are we telling yet?"

"Ours is very…us," Rick hints with a grin.

"I don't want to do ours, but Bella's making me," Sam says, shaking his head.

"Someone's wearing a dress," Jimmy teases.

Merry grins. "I'm not telling you what I'm coming as, but you'll definitely know it's me."

"Are you wearing the mermaid tail, Marina?" Beth asks.

"Eek, no. That horrible thing is framed and hanging on the wall in my office at The Mermaid Foundation. It will never terrorize me again."

Zach sneaks up behind her and kisses the top of her head.

"As I recall, it didn't work out so badly the last time you wore it."

She grins up at him and accepts a kiss.

"No, it sure didn't."

The conversation slips easily into small talk, and my mind wanders again, back to that beautiful house. I'd wrap the handrails of that gorgeous porch in a garland of fall foliage. Pumpkins and gourds of all sizes would line the steps, and I'd arrange more on either side of the door. One of the large trees that's close to the house looked perfect for hanging a swing. I can just imagine spring and summer evenings there. I'll bet the sunset makes everything glow beautifully.

"What are you thinking about?" Rick murmurs against my hair.

I shake my head. "Nothing important. Did you check your costume yet?"

He laughs under his breath. "I did. There are no dents or dings. We're good to go."

I grin and wiggle excitedly in my spot. "Perfect. I can't wait to see their faces."

Later, a small group of us are walking from shop to shop in town. Max came with us, but he is at a local coffeehouse with Gabi, as going for a walk isn't entirely practical for him and his crutches. We're approaching Wallaby's, which is the store where Gabi works, and I give it a look from the outside. It looks like an old-fashioned drug and general store, complete with a soda fountain.

"I think that's where Gabi works," Scarlet says from my left.

I nod. "Yep, it is. Looks like a cute place."

Rick has taken an interest in it as well, but I'm surprised when he steps away and lets go of my hand. I look up at him in silent question.

"I just want to go in and quickly grab something," he tells me. "Where are we headed again?"

"Lu Lu's Pie Shop just up the street," Marina replies.

We've walked off our taco buffet from earlier, and now we plan to celebrate with pie. I love this plan. I step towards Rick.

"I can go with you if you want."

He waves a hand. "No, no, I'll just be a minute. Stay with the group and I'll catch up."

When I frown at him, he kisses me on the temple.

"I promise."

I nod and let Scarlet tug me away as Rick disappears into Wallaby's. Scarlet loops an arm through mine.

"What was that about?" she asks.

I'm glad to have her all to myself for a moment. Andrew is up in the front of the group with the guys, and from the sound of things, they're teasing him about his awesome karaoke skills. I shake my head at Scarlet.

"I don't know, but he was acting weird earlier, too," I tell her. "Not in a bad way, necessarily. You know that feeling you get when someone's not giving you all the information?"

She nods.

"Like that. I feel like he's plotting, but I don't know what it could possibly be."

"Okay, but Rick plotting isn't like some creepy dude plotting."

We both laugh, and I nod enthusiastically.

"Absolutely right," I tell her. "If Rick is plotting, it can only be good. And I'm here for it."

Merry steps away from Bella and comes to my other side, looping her arm through my free one. She bobs her chin at us both.

"Can I talk you guys into going into the cookware shop with me?"

I don't even have to think about it.

"Absolutely. It's right by the candle shop, right?"

"Are you going to buy more candles? You're almost as obsessed as Beth," Scarlet asks incredulously, laughing.

"No, I think I have enough candles to make it through a month-long blackout," I tell her. "I'm just referring to it for navigational purposes."

The next shop we pass is a boutique for women, and there's a beautiful scarf in the window. The various shades of blue, purple, and lavender are so eye-catching. I'm happy to see that Beth, who's just behind the guys with Marina, stops and wants to go inside.

The guys decide to wait outside for us. As soon as we go in, I head to the small stack of those scarves that are on display in the window. It's not like I absolutely need a new scarf, but it's so pretty. I check the price and am happy to see it fits in my budget. Marina and Scarlet are done looking almost immediately, and they head back out to join the guys. I pluck a scarf off the top of the display pile and head towards the back of the shop to see what else is there.

Beth and Bella are looking at a jacket on the sale rack as I pass. I don't really see anything else that looks interesting, but I'm also looking for Merry. I didn't see her walk by on her way to the door. At the far back of the shop, there's an orange velvet chaise outside the dressing rooms. This is where I find Merry, sitting by herself, looking thoughtfully at some jack-o'-lantern pajamas. I step over and take a seat next to her.

"Whatcha doing?" I ask. "Contemplating some Halloween jammies?"

She doesn't answer right away. She just keeps staring at the display.

I gently nudge her knee with mine, and she startles and looks over at me.

"Sorry," she mutters. "Just doing my brain laundry."

Okay. This kind of comment isn't unusual for Merry. Not at all. But I can't quite connect the dots. She sees this in my confused expression.

"You know...separating my thoughts into light and dark."

A laugh bubbles up out of me, and I wrap an arm around her shoulders.

"I love you, dude," I tell her. "You okay?"

She nods and stands. "Yep. Always. Let's roll."

I stand and follow her to the checkout counter. "Let's roll."

I pay for my purchase quickly, and there's still no Rick when we get outside. I look down the sidewalk, and there's no sign of him. What could he need at Wallaby's that's taking this long?

Next, we head inside the cookware shop that Merry wanted to check out. She's like a kid in a candy store as soon as we step inside. Her eyes make one sweep across the entire floor, and she grabs a handbasket from a rack near the door. Something tells me we're going to be in here a while.

I'm not big on kitchen gadgets, but I start at the window and walk along the various wooden display tables and shelves. There are stoneware and cast-iron pans of all shapes and sizes. There's a large wooden hutch against the wall with basket after basket displaying all different shapes of cookie cutters.

Next is a display of baking tools. There are bins of rolling pins, cookie sheets, and other baking paraphernalia. There's a large glass bowl containing a bunch of whisks...and they're so pretty. My hand drifts to one almost on its own, and I hold it up in the light. It's a big one, and it's made of copper, so it's attention-getting. How pretty.

I stand there for a moment, just turning it around and around so the copper catches the light. Just next to the whisks, there's a stand mixer that's the same copper color. Also gorgeous. I smile to myself as I imagine baking Christmas cookies in that kitchen on Autumn Lane with Rick and our children.

"That's gorgeous," Beth says from beside me. "Do you like to bake?"

I smile and put the whisk back, suddenly feeling silly for obsessing about the house again.

"I do, but not like Merry," I tell her. "I just thought it was pretty."

Beth nods. "I can't really cook. Jimmy and I are going to take cooking classes together when we travel."

I smile at her. "That's wonderful. Then you'll have all these memories to cherish after you get back home. Every time you cook pasta, you'll remember how you learned to make it in Italy."

Beth nods. "Exactly."

She moves over to a display of cookbooks just as Merry whizzes past. I'm in shock at the amount of stuff in her basket already. I laugh under my breath. The bell above the door rings, and a Viking god walks in. His eyes immediately find mine, and he smiles, slowly walking through the displays until he's standing at my side. I spring up on my toes and give him a kiss.

I look around for a bag from Wallaby's, but he's empty-handed.

"They didn't have what you needed?"

He kisses the tip of my nose. "They did."

I wait for him to elaborate, but he just stares at me with a twinkle in his eyes.

"Rick, you're up to something again," I whisper, waiting for an answer.

He smiles again, and it's just the most beautiful thing. My heart swells with love. He looks at the display table beside me.

"What were you looking at over here?"

I give him an exasperated look, then turn back to the copper whisks and pull one out. I twirl it in front of him.

146

"Aren't these beautiful?"

He nods. "They are. Not as beautiful as my Fireball."

I laugh softly, and he reaches out and takes my hand.

"Do you want to know what I'm up to?"

I grin. "More than anything."

He gently tugs on my hand. "Come with me."

I squeal under my breath as Rick leads me out the door and onto the sidewalk. There's a crowd that's gathered. The Headless Horseman is here. A man dressed all in black on a huge black horse is slowly moving along the street. He has a large plastic jack-o'-lantern in his hand with fake flames billowing out of it. It looks amazing.

Rick pulls me down the sidewalk and away from the crowd. There's a bench in front of the pie shop and we sit. He wraps an arm around my shoulders and pulls me in close, then pulls a small white box from his coat pocket and places it in my hand.

"For you."

I look down at the small box in confusion. Did he buy me a ring at Wallaby's? That can't be. They're a drug store, general store, and hardware store combination. I went in there once with Marina. I never saw a jewelry counter.

"What did you do?" I ask, searching his handsome face.

"Open it."

I balance the little box on my leg and pull the glove off my left hand, wiggling my ring finger.

"You already bought me the best ring ever," I tease. "What is this?"

He just grins. "Open it."

I set my glove in my lap and pick up the box. Now that I look at it closer, it's a little bit bigger than a ring box. I give Rick one last look before pulling the lid off the box and peering inside.

It's a silver key blank.

I frown at him. "A key?"

"Look inside the lid."

I'm still holding the box lid, so I turn it over and gasp. I look up at Rick with tear-filled eyes.

"What does this mean?"

He laughs softly and kisses me. "I think you've figured it out pretty well."

I look down at the inside of the box lid and the tiny photo of the house on Autumn Lane that's glued there. I shake my head.

"Did you buy this house?" I choke out in a whisper.

"I did."

"Rick!" I exclaim. A tiny sob escapes my throat, but I just keep staring at the picture.

"Before you scold me," he says sweetly. "Consider it an early wedding gift."

I swallow hard, then laugh. "I was going to get you new cuff links or something. I can't compete with a house."

"You don't have to get me anything, baby," he says. "But I'm sure I'll love them."

I shake my head again.

"What about San Francisco?" I ask. "What about Daddy?"

He takes the box and lid from me, setting them on the bench, then takes both my hands in his.

"There's no rush to move here," he assures me. "You saw the inside. It needs a lot of updates. We'll live in San Francisco while we do that, and as long as you want, when it's done. We can stay in San Francisco as long as you want, and use this one for weekend getaways. And if you decide you *never* want to live here, we'll just sell it."

I wrap my arms around Rick's neck and press my lips to his. Again. And again. And again. He pulls me into his lap with one deft move. I kiss him again, but this time it's softer. Slower. Finally, I pull away and press our foreheads together.

"I love you so much," I tell him.

"I love you too, Fireball."

I reach down and pull the key from the box.

"This isn't actually the key to the house," I say. "There's no way you'd get it that quickly."

Rick laughs and holds the box so I can put the key back and close the lid.

"I wasn't sure how to give it to you, so I went into Wallaby's and asked them to print the picture. Then I found the gift box. I was just going to take a key off my key ring, but they had these blanks in the hardware section."

I laugh under my breath. "So creative."

"I have to be if I'm going to keep up with you."

I nudge him in the side. "Thank you. I can't wait to live in that house with you."

Rick's eyes are full of love as his gaze flicks over my face.

"I thought we could offer the guest cottage to your dad," he says.

If there's any more emotion squeezing on my ribs, I may faint. I can't believe this man's generous heart. I nod, swallowing hard again. Words are lost to me right now.

"So I have one more question for you, Fireball," he says.

I look up into his handsome face and smile brightly.

"And what's that?"

He grins mischievously. "Should we go back inside and buy that whisk for the kitchen?"

I burst into laughter, and so does he. A happy tear falls down my cheek, and I sweep it away as we stand. He pulls me against his side, and I wrap my arm around his waist.

"Yes," I say, shaking my head in disbelief. "Let's go get that whisk."

IV

Merry

Chapter 10

Merry

"This is the best pie ever," I murmur to Scarlet as I shovel another fork full into my mouth.

"That's a huge compliment coming from such an expert baker," she replies.

I shrug off the compliment. "I'm not really a pie baker, though. I'm more about cookies and cake. And tiramisu, of course."

"Well, since I only know how to bake if it involves a box or a tube of raw dough, I stand by my statement."

I laugh and give her a half hug, then dig into this delectable wedge of coconut cream goodness on the plate in front of me. My tongue feels like it's on a tropical vacation.

"So you're really not going to call that guy?" Scarlet asks. Her tone is laced with the lightness used when you don't want someone to be mad because you're sticking your nose where it doesn't belong.

I give her a mock glare, but don't answer.

"I mean, he told you how beautiful you are," she continues. "And he sounded cute."

I put my fork down and face my friend.

"Yes, he *sounded* cute," I repeat. "Sounded. Because he didn't have a head."

Scarlet scoffs. "He looked pretty fit up on that horse."

I stare at her as if she's grown a second head. Maybe she can loan the headless guy this one.

"I got hit on by the Headless Horseman," I remind her. "He's not even a good guy in literature. The universe couldn't even give me that. Nope. I got hit on by a headless guy."

Scarlet stares at me, and I can tell she's trying not to laugh - so I decide to go all in. I lean in close, eyes big, and whisper. "No head!"

She snort-laughs, and I'm supremely proud of myself. Seriously, though. Marina finds a rockstar. Ashley gets the rockstar's best friend/aka another rockstar. Scarlet's rescued by a muscled-up fireman. And me? Headless. A headless man. That's what I get.

"Honestly, Scarlet, I don't care if he sounded cute," I explain. "He lives all the way across the country from me. I went through that stage a few years ago. One date, maybe two, and next please! I don't want to just go on dates and have fun. I want to go on dates with my *person*."

She nods. I know she gets it. Actually, all my girls get it. Marina was dead set on running away from Zach as fast as she could when they met. Ashley was positive that Rick only saw her as a friend. And Scarlet was determined to schedule matters of the heart for a more convenient time. Spoiler alert: it didn't work out that way for any of them. But they remember how they felt when they wanted things the universe wasn't handing them, and that's exactly where I am right now.

When Marina was running from her rockstar, nothing made me happier than my next mistake. I loved the chase. I loved that first date feeling. Sometimes the second date feeling was also pretty great. But after that, I wasn't interested. And now that I actually want to find my person, I catch myself wondering far too often if maybe I met him already…and kicked him to the curb.

What if I had my chance and threw it all away?

It feels true somewhere deep in my heart, and I don't want it to be.

"So what did you get in the cookware shop?" she asks, mercifully changing the subject.

I grin and pull the bag up, setting it on the bench between us. Then I start plucking things out to show her.

"How cute are these Headless Horseman cupcake sprinkles?"

Scarlet takes the little jar from my hand to check them out.

"This town is so cool," she says, putting the jar on the table. "I love how much they lean into all the Headless Horseman stuff."

"I also got some Christmas stuff," I say, setting three more shakers on the table.

One jar contains little pink Santas, one has reindeer antlers, and one has the word Merry in red sparkles and Christmas in green sparkles.

"So cute."

I spill the rest of the bag out onto the table because I have no shame. Half a dozen jars fall out, all loaded with different colored pearl candies. They're all ball shapes, but varying sizes.

"Ooooh! What will you do with these?"

I grin. "I have absolutely no idea. But some of these colors aren't easy to find. The navy blue ones, especially. I'll save them for something special."

My phone vibrates in my pocket, and I reach for it. It vibrates twice more before I wake the screen, and Scarlet watches curiously.

"Everything okay?"

I nod and give her a crazy smile. "Can you keep a secret?"

She rolls her eyes at me. I hand her my phone. I have the social media app ShutterBug up on my phone, and it's open in my new account. Three more vibrating notifications happen while my phone is in her hand.

The first three photos are of the fall-themed treats I made in Marina's kitchen for our long weekend get-together. The next one is the little cake I made for Jimmy and Beth. I posted them to my account when we left the house. She scrolls even farther back and sees the other stuff I've posted. A cake I made for a little girl's birthday, some custom decorated sugar cookies for a bachelorette party, and my famous Italian wedding cookies.

"The pictures are great, Mer," she says in awe. "Merry's Bakes. That's the name of this account? You're doing social media for it now? This is amazing."

I grin and wiggle around in my seat. "I'm getting so many followers. When we get back to San Francisco, I'm going to update my profile so it reads 'inside Nonno's Italian Bistro in North Beach.'"

Her eyes get huge, and I let out an intentionally maniacal laugh.

"Maybe if Nonno sees how much business I bring in with my baking, he'll start to see what I could turn this into," I say hopefully. "And Christmas is his favorite holiday, too. He's usually all smooshy over me because I'm the grandbaby who was born on Christmas Day. I feel like it might be time for all that."

She nods. "Okay, let me know when I need to be there. Remember, I promised to help you redecorate your nonna's old bakery so he could see. I owe you, my friend."

"Ashley's dad hired Nonno to do in-home catering when he had his group of guy friends over," I tell her. "One of those friends is the mayor, of course. He's hired Nonno to teach an Italian cooking class at a retreat for him, his wife, and their friends. If that happens, he'll be away for at least three days."

"That sounds perfect! And once we get to Thanksgiving, our production shooting breaks, and we won't be working again until after the holidays."

I clap my hands. "Perfect!"

"Well, I guess that's assuming my show gets picked up for another season. I still haven't heard."

I pat her on the shoulder, then set about putting all my purchases back into the bag.

"You will," I say with confidence. "I watch that show every week. You're doing so much good out there. They'd be crazy to cancel it."

Our attention drifts to Rick and Ashley, across the table and down a few spots from us. She laughs out loud at something he says, and he's looking at her like there are no other women on earth. It's both adorable and disgusting.

"They are so cute together," Scarlet says, as if reading my thoughts.

"He bought her a house," I murmur unnecessarily. "How Hallmark movie is that?"

Scarlet grins. "They're so meant for each other. It's adorable."

"It is."

We were all together when they came bursting into the pie shop to meet us and told us the news. Everyone rushed over to hear the story. Marina and Zach are, of course, thrilled that they'll be neighbors whenever they're in New York. I smile softly and feel those all too familiar *why not me* vibes trying to come in.

There may be a little jealousy there, which is human. But it's mostly frustration, and not just to do with the fact that I only seem to meet men who are clearly not marriage material. Nonno, my grandfather, is still stubbornly denying my request to reopen my Nonna's bakery. It's my biggest dream. Like, I could even learn to be happy without my person if I just had my cute little bakery next door to Nonno's.

For the longest time, I've known what my ideal life looks like. And yes, it includes an adoring husband and a small busload of kids, but if that never happens for me...the bare bones of the goal have never changed. I want that bakery. I want to bring cheer and love to people through frosting and sprinkles. I want little girls to come in with their parents, squealing in delight over the most awesomely extra unicorn cake that they want for their birthday. I want friends sitting around tables with delicious croissants and cozy mugs of coffee as they catch up with each other on a Saturday morning. I want white walls accented with beautiful, varying shades of pink and a vibe that makes people relaxed and happy just walking in.

So yeah, the dating frustration is real. But my frustration with my grandfather, who is more a father to me than my own father, is so thick I could cut it with a knife. Something has to budge, and it's not going to be me. I'm in it to win it.

"Whatcha thinkin' about?" Scarlet asks with the air of a friend who knows exactly what I'm thinking about. This is becoming a sensitive topic that I don't want to talk about at all, especially around other people who can hear. I give her a smile and dig my fork back into the pie.

"Wondering whether I should buy one of these to go," I lie.

I feel a little bad about it, but not entirely. I know she wants to help. Talking about my dating life nonstop does not help. Actually, it's not nonstop to them. It is to me. First, Marina inserts it into a conversation. Then, when Ashley and I are off together somewhere, it's her turn. Now it's Scarlet's.

Mercifully, she takes a bite of her apple pie and doesn't push. I nudge her, and she nudges back. It's kind of our unspoken language when we don't know what to say to each other. I just told her I'm okay, and she just said I love you. All of that with no words.

"Uh...uh-oh," Scarlet mutters.

I follow her gaze to the front door, where a Headless Horseman with his head showing is now walking across the seating area in the pie shop and making a path straight to me. I look at her for some kind of help, but it's too late. Andrew does a double-take nearby and exchanges looks with Scarlet as if he's wondering how bad this is going to go for the headless guy.

The headless dude pulls out the empty chair across from us and smiles at me. Everyone in our group stops talking so they can watch. Slowly, I make myself meet his gaze.

"Hi," he says.

"Hi."

"I just wanted to show you that I do have a head."

I smile and point my fork at him. "I see that. Thanks for showing me."

He's cute, I have to admit. He has sandy-brown, short hair. Nice green eyes. A kind smile. He seems all right on the surface, but there's a vibe. It's way off. He sits and leans back in his chair like he's going to hang out with me for an hour or two.

Scarlet sits back in her chair and murmurs, "Uh-oh…"

Yep. Red flag number one. I didn't invite you to sit down, dude.

He extends a black-gloved hand to me. "I'm David."

I just don't have it in me to be a dragon lady like Ashley was before Rick romanced her into a better mood. Sometimes I wish I could be more like that and shut a guy down with one word, but I can't.

"I'm Merry," I reply, shaking his hand.

"It's nice to meet you, Merry," he says. "Want to go grab a drink later?"

I take another bite of my pie. "No, but thank you."

"C'mon."

"No, but thank you."

"Is 'no' the only word you can say, Merry? C'mon."

I steal a glance at Scarlet, and she's had enough as well. Sometimes it's good to remind your married friends what they're not missing in the dating world.

"I'm guessing you know that's not true since I've said lots of other words to you tonight, David," I say in a syrupy sweet tone. "But still…no thank you."

He sighs heavily and leans back in the chair.

"I think you're gonna break my heart."

I stick my lower lip out in an exaggerated pout. "I don't think that's true, but I'm real sorry."

He shoots me a grin. "Sorry enough to get me tickets to a Rebels concert as a consolation prize?"

Scarlet gasps and leans over. "Get out right now or you really *will* lose your head."

David scoffs, shoves his way out of the chair, and stomps towards the door. I shake my head as I watch him retreat. What a jerk. Our friends all turn their attention back to their plates.

"Okay, I'm sorry I tried to get you to give him a chance," Scarlet says quietly.

I shrug. "This is what it's like now, my friend. It's just a parade of jerks."

She shakes her head. "There's someone out there who deserves you. I know it."

I look into my friend's eyes, searching. "Maybe. But I don't want to talk about it all the time, okay?"

Her arm comes around my shoulders immediately, and she gives me a squeeze.

"Absolutely," she promises.

I take another bite of my pie and close my eyes, savoring the wonderful flavor and texture of it. It really is the best pie I've ever had.

"Let's go jogging in the morning, okay?" Scarlet suggests. "Just the two of us."

"I still don't understand why anyone runs on purpose and tries to call it fun," I say with a grin. "But sure…if you want to."

She grins excitedly. "Great! We can talk through the decor you want for the bakery. It'll help me be ready to help you when the time comes."

I nod. "It's a date."

The best date I've been offered in quite some time.

***

I wake up and stretch, rolling over and looking out the huge window of the guest room. The sun streams through gauzy curtains because I absolutely refuse to close the drapes when I have such a beautiful view. There's nothing but rolling hills and trees out there, and it's a nice change from my tiny bedroom window in the heart of San Francisco.

I wrap my arms around one of the plush pillows on the bed and hug it against my body. If I could find a way to bring a full kitchen in here, I'd never leave this bed. It is so comfortable. I glance at the clock on the bedside table. I have thirty minutes to change before meeting Scarlet in the kitchen to go jogging. Why did I agree to this?

Because I love my friend and I don't want her to go alone. I know Andrew would go with her if she wanted, but she asked me, and I'm a sucker for my friends.

I roll out of bed, already missing the warm, cozy comfort of the four-poster antique masterpiece behind me. I pad across the room and flick the light on in the bathroom, washing my face with this amazing oatmeal and lavender soap Marina gave me. I brush my teeth, then fuss for a while over what I'm going to wear. With three minutes to spare, I lace up my sneakers and run down the staircase and into the kitchen, where I find not only Scarlet but Marina and Ashley as well.

"Oooh! Are we all going?" I ask hopefully.

Marina laughs out loud.

"No way. But we knew you guys were going, so we came down for a little inner circle bonding before you go."

Ashley sips from a mug and smiles. "These times are getting more and more rare."

Something dips in my gut. She's right, but I hate that she's right. Thankfully, Marina and Ashley still live in the city, just minutes away from me. Scarlet does too, but she travels a lot to film her TV show.

We're all getting so busy that it's harder and harder to meet up.

"Coffee?" Marina asks me.

I shake my head. "I don't think marathon runners go running with a belly full of coffee. How about a water?"

They all laugh softly, and Marina grabs a bottle of water from the fridge. She hands it to me, and I sit on one of the barstools around the island. A thump sounds upstairs, and Marina makes a face.

"I'm having such a great time, but I'd love a weekend of just us four," she says quietly. "Can we make that happen soon?"

"A whole weekend?" Ashley croons. "That would rock."

I flip the cap on my water and take a swig, then nod. "I'm in."

"Me too," Scarlet says. "Which may be easier for me if my show isn't renewed."

"Hey, it will be," Ashley says sweetly. "There's no way they don't renew it."

"Do you guys want anything to eat before you go?" Marina asks.

I shake my head and look at Scarlet. "I don't. You?"

"Nah," she says with a wink. "I hear marathon runners don't eat before they run."

"Tease me all you want," I joke. "You don't know."

Scarlet laughs. "Are you planning a career as a marathon runner?"

I jump off the stool and jog in place a few times. "Gotta think big, girl!"

Their laughter is my reward, as usual. I live for a good laugh. I pull myself back up on the stool and take another swig of water.

"So how long are you guys going to end up living on this side of the world?" Scarlet asks Marina and Ashley. There's a hint of longing in her voice.

Marina shakes her head. "Honestly, I don't think it'll be a lot. Zach was used to touring with the band before he met me, and he only stayed here during their breaks."

Ashley nods. "Rick and I talked it through last night. He bought it for me as a surprise, because he saw how much I loved it, but he knows I don't want to live this far away from my dad. We'll be in San Francisco most of the time, but it's fun to have a retreat to go to."

I shake my head and whistle.

"What?" Scarlet asks.

I nod my head at Ashley and Marina. "These rich girls and their retreat homes."

We all laugh, and Scarlet winks at me.

"Thank goodness they'll continue to invite us to their palatial estates for parties."

Ashley rolls her eyes at us. "Oh, whatever."

Marina grins and points at me. "Best baker ever."

This is a game we play sometimes, when we just want to cheer each other on. I nod and point at Ashley.

"Best teacher and children's book author ever."

Now it's Ashley's turn to point to Scarlet.

"Best interior designer ever."

Scarlet wiggles a finger at Marina. "Best philanthropist ever and still the best singing voice of all four of us."

We all share another laugh. Marina's phone rings, and she pulls it from her pocket.

"Oh! It's Hillary," she tells us. "Hang on."

She swipes to answer and holds the phone to her ear.

"Hey, Hills, I—"

Marina's expression turns grave, and we all get quiet.

"What? Oh no! Well, why didn't she call me?"

Scarlet, Ashley, and I exchange curious looks.

"Ugh," Marina groans. "I hate this so much. She's never a bother."

Ashley pulls a stool out for Marina, motioning her to sit, and she does. We move closer, and I put a reassuring hand on her shoulder.

163

"Okay, sure," she says in a voice that's growing thick with emotion. "Okay. Yep. No, you can call us anytime, too. But thank you for getting up early to let me know. I'll send her a text to call me when she wakes up."

More silence.

"Okay, thank you so much, Hillary."

Marina's eyes fill with tears as soon as she disconnects the call.

"Livvie had a bad day at school yesterday," she chokes out. "Some kids are bullying her. They know she's in foster care, and they teased her about not being wanted. She's been going to the Mermaid Foundation office after school until her foster mom picks her up after work, and Hillary noticed something was wrong. She got the story out of her."

Ashley lets out a frustrated sigh. "And she didn't call you? That's not like her."

"Apparently, these kids told her that we're all just being nice to her so it looks good to other people, but we don't really care and she's a burden," Marina continues, wiping away a tear. "The same thing happened to me when I was in foster care, but I was older."

"That's so cruel," Scarlet murmurs.

"Hillary said it bothered her all night, but Livvie's foster mom didn't want to bother us with it while we're out here. I hate this."

"Hey, no one's going to get mad if you need to go back to California," Ashley says sweetly.

Marina shakes her head. "No, that won't solve anything at this point. And there are rules. Even though Miranda has been great when it comes to including us, we can't just show up on her porch and ask to see Livvie."

"I'm so sorry this is happening to her," I tell her. "Is there anything we can do to help?"

Marina forces a smile. "No, but thank you. I think these things hit me harder because they remind me of an awful time in my life, and I don't ever want a child to have to go through what I did."

Scarlet nods solemnly. "Of course."

"Where's Zach?" Ashley asks.

"He's still upstairs."

Ashley opens her arms. Scarlet and I get the message. We get up and pull Marina into a group hug. For a while, we just stand there together, wrapped around her and hugging each other.

"I really love you guys," she squeaks out.

We hug for a few more moments, and then we begin to gently let go. Ashley takes her by the shoulders.

"Alright, now you go upstairs and tell Zach what's happened," she says. "I'll stay down here and let Maggie and her team in when they arrive. You take whatever time you need."

"We can help too," Scarlet chimes in, and I nod in agreement.

"I'll be fine for a bit on my own," Ashley tells us. "You're not actually marathon runners. You'll be back soon enough."

Scarlet and Marina both nod.

"Thanks, you guys," Marina says, wiping away another tear. "I'll be down soon."

"No," I say gently. "You'll be down when you're ready, and we'll handle everything in the meantime."

A genuine smile from her this time. She gives each of us a hug and then heads upstairs to talk to Zach.

"We really can stay behind and help," I offer to Ashley.

Scarlet huffs. "You just don't want to go jogging."

"No one wants to go jogging," I tell her, barely stifling a laugh.

Scarlet smirks at me.

"Well, now we're going just because you said that."

I stick my tongue out at her, making Ashley laugh.

"Get out of here, ladies," she says. "I'll hang right here, and then we can figure things out. I'm sure everything will be all right once she and

Zach have a chance to talk things through."

"I think so too," I tell her, giving her a quick hug.

Scarlet hugs Ashley as well, and we head for the front door.

"If you really don't want to go, Merry, I don't want to make you. It's cool."

I give her a nudge.

"No, I'm okay," I tell her. "I can work off that pie from last night. And maybe I'll actually like it once we get going. Who knows?"

"Yep," she says with a grin. "Who knows?"

Chapter 11

Merry

I don't know how far we've jogged, but I'm pretty sure we're in New Jersey already, and Scarlet says I'm being dramatic. I don't think so. Okay, maybe a little.

The jog through Marina's neighborhood was beautiful. Winding, tree-lined streets and little pockets of woods are tucked in between impressive homes. And it's so quiet here. It's not like San Francisco at all, which is kind of nice for a while. Now we're at the edge of town, so we're waiting at the crosswalk, and my lungs are on fire. I bend over while we wait for the light to change.

"You should walk in place," Scarlet suggests. "It's better if you don't stop moving completely."

I stick my tongue out at her because I'm too winded to really argue with my typical flourish. I don't miss the fact that she's pressing her lips together, so she doesn't smile. Or laugh. Both would be horrible mistakes right now.

"Are you giving me cranky looks because you hate jogging or because you're worried about Marina?"

I nod. "Yes."

The light changes, and we jog across, continuing up the sidewalk as the cute little shops begin to appear. This area is so charming it could be on a postcard. Shop windows are filled with all different types of goods for sale, and several doors are adorned with fall wreaths or spooky garlands. The leaves are really starting to fall now, and the brilliant golds and oranges, and even reds, are everywhere.

"She's got this," Scarlet says. "*They've* got this. Zach and Marina could rule the world."

We stop at the next light, and I hunch over again.

"They'd rock at it."

"If Zach were a citizen, he'd make a great President of the United States, don't you think?" Scarlet muses. "Free concert tickets and tea for all."

"Marina would make a better President," I counter. "And I'd give anything to see Zach as First Gentleman."

Scarlet laughs so hard we have to stop jogging for a minute. So that's the key, huh? Just make her laugh, and I get a break.

"He would just be off to the side all the time, cheering for his mermaid. They're so cute together," she says.

I don't disagree. They're disgustingly adorable. So I have no doubt that they'll figure this thing out with little Livvie.

I spot that cute little cookware shop down the street a bit.

"I wish the shops were open," I tell Scarlet, nodding at the cookware shop. "I wouldn't mind taking another pass at the sprinkles they had."

She chuckles, and we start jogging again when the light changes.

"Dude, where would you carry them?"

I slap my hands on the sides of my leggings, which are printed with various cookies all over them.

"These babies have pockets."

Scarlet laughs as we jog down the sidewalk.

"You're a tiny person," she says. "How many jars of sprinkles could you fit in those things?"

"Ha! These are made of titanium stretchy stuff, my friend. I could fit so many jars in these. It wouldn't even matter if I jogged all the way home with chunky-looking thighs that rattle."

"I love your confidence," Scarlet says, making my heart fill with happy pride. "You really would jog down the street with your leggings overloaded with sprinkles. There's no doubt in my mind about it. And it's just one of the things I love about you, girl."

We stop for another light, and I wrap her in a slightly sweaty hug.

"Love you too," I mutter. "Even when you make me go jogging."

She laughs hard. "Okay, see the church down there?"

I look to where she's pointing and get instantly excited.

"Uh...the Old Dutch Church? From the story? Duh."

"Okay, I don't know what you just said - but why don't we sprint to it, and then we can have a break. Deal?"

I don't even have to think about it. I take off sprinting, causing Scarlet to squeal and laugh. I hear her pounding footsteps behind me and push harder. This may kill me, but it's okay. I'll be at the cemetery already. It'll save some time.

It's so hard not to jerk to a stop when we run across the bridge approaching the church. I saw a sign for Headless Horseman Bridge, but I'm not about to let Scarlet beat me. I run over the bridge and keep going until I get to the iron gates that surround the church and the small parking lot. Scarlet is not far behind.

We both take a minute to catch our breath, walking through the open iron gates and up the sidewalk slowly. Walking into a cemetery, it feels like the weirdest warm-down ever. It's kind of exciting, though. I've wanted to check out this place all weekend, and we never quite made it far enough.

The church comes into better view as we draw closer. The base of the small church is surrounded by fieldstone, with the top third of it covered in white clapboard. There's a small belfry atop the roof that gives it an old-world charm.

"Have you read The Legend of Sleepy Hollow?" I ask Scarlet as we walk.

The sidewalk is on an incline, bringing us up to the same level as the cemetery. I don't wait for an answer as I step onto a path that leads down one line of graves.

"If I have, I don't remember it," she says. "It's possible I read it in school. Have you?"

"Oh, yes," I reply. "More than once. I love Halloween, and the story always feels like part of that to me."

"These graves look so old," she says with reverence.

"They are," I confirm. "The church was built in the late 1600s. It's featured quite a bit in the story."

"It is? All I remember is the Headless Horseman chasing the nerdy school teacher through the woods."

We come to a fork in the path, and I stop, looking at Scarlet with raised eyebrows.

"You're the boss," she says. "I don't care which way we go."

I take a good look around and decide that a left turn, deeper into the cemetery, feels like the thing to do. The path leads just slightly uphill, but it's not very steep.

"I love the way the story's written," I tell Scarlet. "The descriptions of this town and this place are so charming."

"Yeah?"

I nod. "He called it one of the quietest places in the world, and said a drowsy, dreamy influence seems to hang over the land."

"Wow. Poetic."

I nod again and let out a sigh. "No one talks like that anymore. No one takes that kind of trouble to describe things in such a lyrical way anymore."

"Zach might disagree with you on that."

I laugh out loud. I hadn't thought about songwriters, but she's right. "Okay, yeah. Zach. Rick. Taylor Swift. They do. But charming little short stories like Sleepy Hollow just don't pop up anymore."

"Romantasy is king right now," Scarlet offers.

I roll my eyes. "Romantasy feels more realistic than actual romance right now."

Scarlet stops in her tracks. "I hate that you feel that way."

I shrug and then shudder as if trying to shed the last dozen horrible dates I had before I declared my self-imposed dating hiatus a few months ago. Too handsy, too apathetic, too creepy, too much in one way or another. I felt like Goldilocks, looking for something just right but having a real hard time finding it.

"Is it that bad out there?" Scarlet asks gently.

I smirk. "The dating pool needs a little chlorine in it."

A laugh bubbles up out of me, and then I snort. Scarlet laughs and shakes her head.

"I'm sorry, I shouldn't laugh."

I shake my head. "No, it's okay. It's always better to laugh than cry."

We keep walking up the path, our silence giving way to the sounds of the surrounding woods making themselves known. Off in the distance, a little gray squirrel scampers down a hill and up a tree.

"It really is beautiful here," I say. "The woods, the river, the charming little shops. It's so different from home."

Scarlet nods. "It is. I'm a city girl, though. I can't see myself ever living in a place like this. Marina has to drive thirty minutes just to go to Target."

I smirk. "What a tragedy."

Scarlet laughs. "Whatever."

We keep walking until we crest the gentle hill, and my attention is grabbed by a small gate with the name Irving on top of it.

"Oh my gosh," I exclaim as I step closer. "I'd forgotten Zach told me about this!"

Scarlet's eyes are wide. "About what?"

"Washington Irving is actually buried in this cemetery."

"Oh wow, you're kidding," she replies. "That's pretty cool, actually. Which one is his?"

I look around the many graves behind the gate. There are so many headstones of Irving ancestors, but one of the bigger headstones has an American flag on it with two small pumpkins. *Washington Irving* is engraved into the stone. Wow. This is amazing. I point to it.

"There he is. Wow. This is so cool."

Scarlet grins down at me as I take a seat on the stone steps just below the gate.

"I never knew you were such a geek for this story."

I smile up at her. "I re-read the story just before this trip. I wanted to have it fresh in my mind when we were walking around town."

She nods, and we grow silent again as we take a moment to look at the beauty of this old cemetery. I hear a stirring of something. Some leaves crunching, maybe. Behind me. I turn to look, and there's nothing out of order. Then I hear it.

"Did you hear that?" I ask Scarlet as I look around for the source.

"Hear what?"

I don't bother answering at first. I stand up and turn to look behind me. I swear I heard a tiny little cry.

"Merry, wha—"

"Ssh! I heard it again."

Scarlet's eyes are huge as she watches me. I step up the little stone steps and lean over the gate as far as I can. I'm sure it was behind me.

"What are you doing?"

"Looking for something I hope I don't find."

"What?"

"Sssh!" I say again. "I think I heard a little cry."

Now Scarlet's on the stone steps beside me, leaning over.

"What's crying? Something we're going to have to run from?"

Still peering into the small hillside of headstones, I shake my head.

"No, like a—"

Mew. *Mew.*

"Oh my gosh, I hear it too," Scarlet says.

And there it is...poking out from behind Washington Irving's headstone: a tiny black fuzzy head. A kitten.

"Hey, baby!" I call out. "Pspspsps."

Scarlet pspsps as well. The kitten waddles across the grass towards us, mewing louder than a full-grown cat. I reach my hand through the gate and run my fingers through the grass.

"Come here, baby," I say softly. "Come on."

The kitten sniffs the air. He's so tiny. He has to be just barely weaned from his mother. I wiggle my hand in the grass again, and he runs for me, mewing loudly the whole way until he literally pounces into my palm. I gently close my hand around his little body and pull him through the gate.

"Oh my gosh, little dude," I say as I draw him against my chest. "It's so cold out here. Are you okay?"

He begins purring immediately as I sit back on the stone steps and cradle him in my lap. Scarlet sits beside me, making dorky little cooing noises at him and rubbing his little forehead with her finger. He bites at the air around her finger, and I laugh.

I look him over for injuries and don't see any. He keeps mewing, though, which makes me think he's probably hungry. I look over at Scarlet.

"We should get him some food and water," I say. "He looks okay now, but who knows how long he's been out here alone."

She nods, and we stand up.

"Poor little guy," she says as we walk back down the path we came up. "He's so young, though. I hope there aren't any litter mates out there still."

"I didn't hear anything else, but the church door was open when we came in. Maybe we can tell someone to keep an eye out."

Suddenly, I get an idea and hand the kitten to Scarlet.

"Hold him for a sec."

I pull off the hoodie I have on over my t-shirt and put it on backwards so the hood is hanging over my chest. Scarlet watches me with a frown as if I've lost my mind. I take the kitten back and put him in the hood, drawing the strings just slightly until he has a safe and warm little hammock. Scarlet shakes her head in wonder.

"Genius idea."

I put my hands up under the hood so he gets some warmth from there as well, and we continue walking. I gently massage the little fuzzy bundle through the bottom of the hood, and I'm rewarded with more purring.

We're almost down to the bottom of the slope when I see a groundskeeper's cart pulled over to the side of the path. I look around until I see a man in a green uniform and start flagging him down.

"Excuse me," I call out.

The man smiles and turns our way, stepping carefully across graves until he comes to the path we're on. His eyes immediately go to the little black ball of fur in my hood.

"We found this little guy, and—"

"In the Irving section, I'm guessing?" the man interjects. "I've been looking for him for days."

"Oh! Is he yours?" I ask, ready to scoop him out of my hood. The man holds up a hand to stop me.

"No, no. I trapped all his siblings, but he didn't fall for it. I knew there was a black kitten somewhere, though."

Relief floods in, followed by a flicker of dread when I realize I just got tapped by the Cat Distribution System. I laugh under my breath. How has something so tiny wrapped me around its little paw so quickly?

"Do you want me to take it to the shelter for you?" he asks, and I gasp and step back. He laughs. "It's a no-kill shelter."

"Oh. Sorry," I tell him.

He grins at me. "I think he knew what he was doing when he found you, huh?"

I grin back, then look over at Scarlet.

"That's how the Cat Distribution System works," I tell him.

He furrows his brow, and Scarlet laughs out loud.

"Don't ask, sir," she tells him. "You'll be sorry."

He looks back at me. "There's a pet shop just down the road. Between the bookstore and the cookware shop."

I nod and shoot Scarlet a mischievous grin. Next to the cookware shop, huh?

"Thanks so much."

Scarlet and I step away and walk down the path. I reach into my hood to make sure he's warm enough, and I'm rewarded with more purring.

"So what are you going to name him?" she asks.

"Notta."

She stops in her tracks, staring at me in disbelief. "What?"

"Notta Jogger," I say, cracking up. "No, I'm not sure. Let's think about it."

"That was the worst joke ever," she teases as we step through the iron gates of the church grounds.

"Icky!"

She rolls her eyes. "Okay, it was the ickiest joke ever."

"No! That's what I'm going to name him," I tell her. "Icky Irving."

She frowns at me. "Why on earth would you call this baby Icky?"

"Short for Ichabod," I explain. "And Irving, because he was literally hiding behind Washington Irving's headstone."

"Oh," she replies. "Well, that's actually kind of perfect."

We cross the street with my little friend purring up a storm in my hood.

"Yep. I think so too."

***

An hour later, Scarlet and I walk into the estate with three bags of stuff from the pet store. We head for the kitchen, where we left Ashley. She's there with Beth, chatting at the kitchen island. They both look over at us, and Ashley's eyes nearly pop out of their sockets.

"What on earth? Why is your hoodie on backwards?" she asks as she rushes over to us. "What's in all these bags?"

I open my mouth to explain, and she gasps.

"And why are your leggings so lumpy?"

Oh. I forgot about all the extra sprinkles I picked up after we got Icky all taken care of, and I fed him a little soft food on a bench outside the pet store. Then she sees him in my hood.

"Oh my gosh! Who is this?" she cries.

I pull him out of my hood and show her.

"This is Mr. Ichabod McFluffypants Irving," I say, prompting Scarlet to snort-laugh.

"Dude, you keep adding names."

"I am his *mother*," I say, making a face at her. I turn to Ashley. "Is Marina downstairs yet?"

She nods. "She's in the dining room with most of the others. You're just in time for brunch."

Scarlet puts a hand on my arm. "I'll go get her."

I nod at Scarlet as she heads for the dining room.

"So how's she doing?" I ask.

"She's okay," Ashley explains. "Zach calmed her down, and they talked through it. I'm not sure about the details. Everyone else had started coming down, and it felt weird to ask."

Marina comes in, followed closely by Scarlet. She looks good, which is a relief. She smiles at me.

"What's up?" she asks. "Aren't you hungry after your run?"

Her eyes dip to the kitten in my arms, and she gasps.

"Hello, handsome!" she cries out as she pries him out of my arms and holds him to her cheek. "Oh, he's beautiful!"

In this moment, I find myself feeling a ton of gratitude for the fact that her first reaction is to fawn all over the cutie boy and not worry about why there's a kitten in her pristine house.

"He found me, and now I have to keep him," I tell her. "It's the law."

Scarlet snickers next to me, and I nudge her. Marina laughs.

"Of course you do," she says. "Were you worried I'd make you sleep outside or something?"

I grin at her. "Well, no, but it seemed rude to bring him into your house and not tell you."

Scarlet points to the bags. "She bought out Fido's Finest down on Broadway."

I laugh. "He needed all of that stuff."

"Is there a litter box in there somewhere?" Marina asks.

"Yep. And litter."

She shrugs and hands him back to me.

"Then I have zero problems with this if the litter box stays in your bathroom."

"You're a great friend," I tell her.

"Get him upstairs so you can come down and have brunch with us," she says, then she gasps. "Why are your leggings all lumpy like that?"

"She bought more sprinkles," Scarlet says with a laugh, heading for the French doors. "I'm gonna go grab a quick shower."

177

I nod. "Me too. I'll be down in fifteen."

Marina nods and heads to the dining room with Ashley.

"See you soon, new momma!"

***

Fifteen minutes later, I am not downstairs. I am freshly showered and ready to go, but I seem to be glued to the bathroom floor in my room. I've taken at least twenty pictures of Icky with my cell phone. He's too cute in his little jack-o'-lantern cat bed with his stuffed Headless Horseman toy. I can't tear myself away.

My stomach growls for the dozenth time, and I stand reluctantly. He's passed out on his fluffy bed, not worried about me at all. He has a bit of food left in his bowl and fresh water. He's already used the litter box as well. I put everything in the bathroom so he doesn't claw his way into the bottom of the comfy chair by the bed or disappear into some corner so I can't find him. He's safe, fed, warm, and dry, so it's time for me to get my own breakfast. Or brunch, actually.

I step out of the bathroom and head down the stairs to the dining room, where the entire gang is eating and visiting. Everyone greets me as I wave and rush over to the buffet to start dishing up. I'm heading to an empty seat across from Andrew when Scarlet comes rushing in. I knew better than to take the empty chair next to him, and I grin at him as I sit.

"Wifey's on the way," I say teasingly, and he grins widely.

"How's it going? I heard you're a new mom."

I laugh softly. "He looks just like me. I'm so proud."

Andrew nods and pops a piece of bacon into his mouth.

"Heard that too."

I grab a little pitcher of syrup off the table and pour it over my waffles, making sure I drizzle a little on my piece of fried chicken, too. Next is salt for my potatoes, and I'm ready to dig in. Scarlet comes over with her own plate and gives Andrew a kiss hello.

"Is everyone ready for the big costume party tonight?" Zach asks. "We've got some bloody fabulous prizes for the winners."

Marina grins mischievously next to Zach.

"I can't wait for tonight. This is going to be so fun."

Zach stands, kissing her on the cheek, and grabs two bottles of champagne from an ice bucket on the sidebar. He hands one to Rick and holds the other up.

"Shall we toast to our amazing hostess, friends?"

We all cheer to that as they open the bottles. He and Rick make the rounds, pouring champagne into the flutes that are already on the table. Once we all have champagne, Zach holds up his flute and beams at his wife.

"Marina, my darling Siren," he begins. "Thank you for planning this wonderful weekend for us all...and for putting up with my nonsense. I'm so lucky you're mine."

We all applaud for her as they share a kiss. Then every couple at the table kisses, and I force a smile at the waffle on my plate. This. This right here is what makes me all groany on the inside.

I love that my friends are all happy. I wouldn't change that for the whole world. But that little ping in my gut that happens every time I witness a romantic moment between two people...that gets me. I don't want to feel that anymore. I want to find my person, or I don't want to feel that anymore. It's too much.

"Hey," Scarlet murmurs from across the table. "You okay?"

I smile at her and nod, but I can see she doesn't buy it. I focus on cutting a piece of waffle and putting it in my mouth. I feel that familiar tug of instinct, dragging me into action. It's time to face the inevitable. If I want to find my person, I have to start dating again. I need to find a way to focus on the future, rather than dwelling on past failures. He has to be out there somewhere, and I'm going to start looking again as soon as I get back home.

Chapter 12

Merry

Icky stretches on the bed next to me, making a little cooing noise before putting his tiny paws over his face and going back to sleep. I smirk at him.

"You're supposed to be reading this with me," I tell him, holding up the book as if he's going to understand what I'm saying and look up.

I grab my bookmark and stick it in the book before closing it, mentally cursing Marina for getting me addicted to this thing. *A Throne of Crystal and Stone*? More like *A Throne of Hot Guys and Magic*. But whatever. It's highly entertaining and I can't put it down.

The clock on the nightstand tells me I have ten minutes to get downstairs in costume so the party can start. We're supposed to meet in the haunted library for drinks and appetizers. However, I have no idea how I'm going to drink anything in my costume. Or eat.

Since I have to change, Icky has to go back to his bed in the bathroom. I pick him up and carry him over there, gently laying him down in his pumpkin bed. He doesn't even open his eyes. Adorable. I dump out his water, rinse the dish, put fresh water in it…and leave him to have his peaceful snoozle while I get ready.

Thankfully, I can wear comfy clothes under my costume. I've selected my super special leggings covered in various unicorns that the girls gave me last Christmas. Since I've been dubbed the unicorn of the group, thanks to my positive attitude and unique personality, I've decided to lean in to it. All the way in. I'm also wearing a pink top with a unicorn on it because, why not?

I grab the costume from my suitcase in the closet and lay it out on the floor, making sure the holes I put my feet through are visible and the rest of the costume is spread out flat. Popping my shoes off, I put my feet through the holes and pull the legs up until the elastic around the ankles is in the right place. Then I pull the interior suspenders over my shoulders. I'm fairly petite, so I actually have to cross the suspenders so they form an X across my chest.

Once that's done, I get the battery packs out. I stick one in each pocket of the unicorn leggings, then take the power cords from the costume's fans and plug them into the battery packs. When I'm sure everything is secure, I reach down for the zipper and pull it up until it's just above my chest. Then I turn on the battery packs.

The costume's fans whir to life as I slide my arms into the sleeves and put the pink gloves on my hands. I step over and slip my feet into my shoes, reaching down to make sure the costume's pink hooves cover them. I take a deep breath and pull the rest of the costume forward until it covers my head…and I zip the costume all the way shut.

Just like that, I'm inside a unicorn. I am a unicorn. A giant, inflatable, pink unicorn with a rainbow mane. Epic.

I wait for the costume to finish inflating, then I walk to the bedroom door and open it. Here we go. I get to the landing on top of the stairs and…uh oh. I can't see my feet. I can't see the stairs either.

"Oh my gosh!" I hear Scarlet exclaim.

I pull the costume down so I can see her through the clear window, and she's dressed up like the cutest little bumblebee ever. I wave at her, then beckon for her to come upstairs.

"Help! I can't see my feet."

She snorts, then runs up the stairs to help. I take her hand and keep my other hand on the banister as we slowly descend together.

"You look amazing," she says to me. "This is so cute!"

"You look pretty cute, too," I tell her. "Is Andrew a bee as well?"

We get to the bottom of the stairs, and she turns to me.

"He's a beekeeper!"

I squeal. "I can't wait to see that! Let's go."

I can't really see anything but what's straight in front of me, but when Scarlet walks me into the library, a bunch of people let out gasps, squeals, and various joyful noises. I think I got 'em with this one.

"That can't be anyone but Merry!" I hear Ashley say behind me.

I turn and find her entering the library behind us in the cutest green mini dress. She has matching knee-high green boots on, and there are dragon wings coming out of the back of her dress. Wow. Our dragon lady has come to life, and Rick is wearing a full suit of armor. I jump up and down and clap my pink-gloved hands when I see him. He bursts out laughing. The inflatable costume is wiggling like a giant force field of jelly, so I'm sure I look ridiculous. Mission accomplished.

Marina rushes up to me, dressed as a cowgirl.

"You look so cute!" I exclaim through the plastic window.

She hugs me, which forces the air inside the suit to move elsewhere. My tail hits someone and I hear Sam laugh.

"Watch out for that rainbow butt!"

Zach comes over to say hi. He's dressed as a cowboy as well, which totally tracks because he's obsessed with the American cowboy. I see Andrew, dressed in a full beekeeper's suit, talking to Jimmy and Beth, who are completely decked out in goth attire. But it's really Sam and Bella who steal my heart. She is dressed in a full bear suit, and Sam is dressed as Goldilocks. Blonde pigtails, red ribbons in his hair, blue pinafore dress, and little black patent leather shoes with lacy socks. And big hairy legs. It's hysterical.

The excellent waitstaff are back tonight. The spooky bar, the creepy bartender, all of it. I take my giant inflatable body over to the bar and order a margarita, then I carefully maneuver my way over to the sofas at the back of the library. Scarlet catches up with me.

"You're going to have to unzip if you're going to drink that," she says.

I hand her my drink and pull the zipper down until it's over my chest, then I poke my head out of the opening. I smile at her and take my drink back. When I sit, all the air in the suit rushes up out of the opening, and my hair flies up in my face. Scarlet and I nearly die from laughter, and Marina heads over to see what's up. As soon as she sees me, she starts cracking up.

Scarlet snaps a photo of me with her phone and holds it up, making me snort. I look silly with this thing on the regular way, but now I have a giant inflatable body and a normal head poking out up top. I laugh, shrug it off, and take a sip of my margarita.

Beth comes and sits with us, and I shake my head in wonder at her face full of metal. Her eyebrows have spikes over them, her nose is suddenly pierced, and her chin has a bolt coming out of it. I point at her face and move my finger in a circle.

"How did you do all that? It looks amazing."

She laughs and strikes a pose. "Magnets and glue, friends."

There are chips and four different kinds of salsa on the coffee table, so I dish some up and dig in. Scarlet eyes me curiously.

"Did you hold Icky after you put that thing on?"

I shake my head. "No, why?"

She makes a claw with her hand. "He could put a hole in it."

I grin. "He would never. He's a momma's boy."

"I love that you found a black cat at Washington Irving's grave," Beth says. "On Halloween, even. It was meant to be."

"It certainly seems that way," I agree.

"Psst!" Ashley says as she runs over to us. "Max and Gabi are here."

Marina's face lights up as she stands and whirls around. We all turn our heads to see Gabi dressed as Dorothy from The Wizard of Oz and Max in a very fun, very homemade tin man costume.

"Aren't they just the cutest thing ever?" Ashley says quietly, a sweet smile on her face as she watches them.

They really are adorable. They're still staring at each other like they're the only people on the planet. Too bad, though. They're going to have to take their eyes off each other long enough to appreciate this inflatable monstrosity.

I stand and make quick work of getting myself back in the suit. Then I wait back here with the girls while Max and Gabi make their rounds, saying hello and exchanging praise over each costume they see.

Finally, they make their way back to us. Max takes one look at me and bursts out laughing while Gabi runs over to take a photo with me. She has the best giggle, and she can't stop fussing over the rainbow mane on my costume…so I keep wiggling around for her. Max takes a seat in an oversized chair across from me while I unzip and deflate enough to sit back down.

"This is so cool," Gabi says as she gestures around the library. "Thank you so much for inviting me."

Marina smiles at her, and I have to stifle a laugh. I know my friend, and she'd love nothing more than to squirrel Gabi away into a corner and pelt her with a million questions. Not in a bad way. In an *oh-em-gee, you like my brother, and I want to know all the things about you,* way.

"Gabi, there are soft drinks and cocktails at the bar, and please help yourself to some appetizers," Marina tells her. "Dinner isn't for an hour."

Gabi moves to Max's side. "Thanks so much."

I'm trying not to stare. I'm so happy for Max. But it's really hard not to just sit back and watch these two with a stupid grin on my face. I don't want to embarrass him, though, so I take another sip of my margarita.

"Gabi, that's a great costume," I tell her. "You make a cute Dorothy."

"Thank you so much," she replies. "I already had it, so when Max suggested he go as another Wizard of Oz character, I was really happy."

"It's perfect," Ashley says.

"Do you want anything to drink?" Gabi asks Max. "I'm going to get something."

"Whatever soda is fine, thanks, babe."

Marina shoots us a secret look from behind Max. She is really eating this up. She schools her expression to a neutral one, and she joins Beth on the couch.

"So why did you pick the tin man?" Marina asks her brother.

He sits back and grins like a lovesick puppy. "*She* picked the tin man. She said it was because I have the best heart."

"Aww!" Beth croons.

"Beth, you look incredible," Max tells her. "Those piercings look so real."

Marina looks over her shoulder, I suspect to see where Gabi is, then she turns back to Max.

"You *do* have the best heart. So how's it going?"

Max laughs under his breath.

"Take it easy, sis. She has a family thing to go to tomorrow, so I'll give you all the details at breakfast. Does that work?"

She beams at him. "I'll try to be patient until then."

Max shakes his head and laughs as Gabi returns with drinks for both of them. He scoots over immediately so she can wedge herself into the same chair. Freaking adorable.

I load up a tortilla chip with salsa and pop the whole thing in my mouth. Then I chase it with a sip of margarita. Heaven.

"Okay, Gabi," I say, shoving my giant rainbow tail a little more behind me. It's starting to drive me nuts. "How's the dog rescue going?"

Gabi beams at us, and Max reaches over and laces their fingers together.

"It's amazing," she replies. "I'm using my grandfather's property for it. He has a beautiful old farmhouse on ten acres. There are two barns that can be easily updated so they can be used as kennels, which I have my brothers working on."

"How many brothers do you have?" Bella asks.

"Five," she says with a cute little grimace. "And I'm the youngest, so they're all impossible. But they love me and they're very excited for me."

"No one's more excited than Kirby," Max chimes in.

"Who's Kirby?" Marina asks.

Gabi laughs softly. "Kirby is a very precocious Saint Bernard who will be the first guest at the rescue. She's currently staying in the farmhouse with me."

Max gives her a skeptical look.

"I'm pretty sure that's where she's staying," he says sweetly. "She's your first foster fail. There's no way you're not keeping her as a pet."

Gabi's expression is so guilty. "Yeah, maybe."

"You should have brought her with you," Ashley says. "I love big dogs."

"Oh wow, I would never do that around all the food and drinks," Gabi says, laughing. "She needs some training."

Max nods. "She ate an entire box of donuts yesterday when we weren't looking."

"Oh no!" Marina exclaims. "Did she get sick?"

Gabi shakes her head. "Not only did she not get sick, but when I scolded her, she looked proud of herself. She wasn't sorry at all."

She pulls out her cell phone and shows us pictures. What a gorgeous dog. I don't see how Gabi's ever going to give her away to someone. I agree with Max…this is a total foster fail. She has as many pics of this dog as I do of Icky.

"I just want to say thank you again for what you did," Gabi says to Marina. "I was already bowled over when Max walked in with a whole group of you to try to win the prize, but then when you stepped up and donated to everyone…that was the most generous thing I've ever seen."

Marina smiles at her fondly. "People who do good in this world should have good things happen to them. Zach and I were very happy to help."

By the time dinner rolls around, this is absolutely the weirdest thing I've ever experienced. We look like some kind of motley, crazy bunch from a David Lynch movie. Sam's blonde pig tails were driving him nuts, so he slipped off the wig and wrapped them around his neck like a scarf. Bella sits beside him, still wearing the bear suit but without a head. Andrew's beekeeper helmet disappeared hours ago, and Scarlet's bee antennae took a dive in the apple bobbing barrel on the deck. Zach and Marina are still pretty put together, but they're missing their hats. The only thing left of Rick's suit of armor is the shoulders and boots. Everything else has either fallen off or been taken off during the party. Ashley has a bent dragon wing, but is otherwise holding up just fine. And Beth and Jimmy can't stop laughing because the glue is wearing off on some of their fake piercings, and they keep landing in their salads. And me? One of my battery packs ran out of juice about an hour ago, so one side of my unicorn butt was looking luscious and the other was very droopy. I turned off the battery packs and the whole thing looks like some kind of pink plastic jumpsuit.

Zach taps his wine glass with a knife, the light clanging noise bringing the entire dining room to silence. He takes Marina's hand and squeezes it.

"Friends, we have a bit of an announcement to make," he says to the room.

We all exchange excited looks as Marina nods at Zach to share their news.

"Over the past few months, you've all become aware of our special relationship with one of the children that Marina met through an event the Mermaid Foundation hosted" he says. "Livvie has become special to us both. She's in a good foster home now, but it isn't a permanent situation because the foster parent only does temporary placements. So Marina and I have decided to put in our application to become official foster parents and, if Livvie is agreeable to it, we'll become her foster parents."

The entire room erupts in cheers and well-wishes. Ashley wipes a tear from her cheek.

"And then you'll adopt her?" she asks with a hopeful air.

Marina nods happily. "If she'll have us, yes."

"Oh, she absolutely will," I pipe in. "This is the best idea ever. You would be such a great mom, Marina!"

Everyone applauds, and then we take turns hugging the future new parents. I can't believe it. By spring next year, Marina could be a mother and Ashley will be married. Scarlet's already married. Who knows…maybe she'll be pregnant. And here I am still fighting my grandfather to open my dream bakery.

I shove my negative thoughts aside. I'm so tired of them. I would much rather be happy than sad or worried. I've been in a funk, and it's time to snap out of it.

"And Ashley, how are the wedding plans going?" Bella asks.

Ashley's face lights up with love as she looks at Rick and then back at Bella.

"We've done all the big things except for dresses," she says. "The wedding will be at the Palace of Fine Arts with a grand reception in

Golden Gate Park. Flowers, food, music—they're all set."

Marina smiles at her. "We'll have so much fun dress shopping."

"Dress shopping?" I tease. "Can't I just wear my unicorn suit?"

Everyone laughs. I'm actually looking forward to dress shopping. I know Ashley will choose something absolutely stunning, and she'll make sure we love our bridesmaid dresses.

I hear a vibrating noise and look over at Scarlet just in time to see her jump in her seat. Her phone is on the table, and Andrew lights up, wrapping an arm around her as she checks her messages.

"You guys!" she cries out. "My show just got renewed!"

I squeal with excitement, joining in the applause for my friend. Andrew pulls her into his arms and plants a kiss on her temple as she sighs in relief.

"Did you really think there was a chance it wouldn't go through?" I ask her. "What kind of human cancels a show like that? You're out there doing good for people."

She shrugs. "You never know until it happens for sure. That's what I've learned. I'm so grateful."

"Is your schedule going to be as crazy this time?" Marina asks.

"Nope, and I'm so happy about that," Scarlet says. "I'll have more creative control, and I managed to get Brad and Kayla on as producers. So they'll still be on camera with me, working on the projects, but now they'll be able to add the role of producer to their resumes."

"Not to mention the fatter paycheck," Rick chimes in.

She nods. "Exactly."

"Whatever happened to Sarah, your other friend that you were designing with?" Ashley asks.

Scarlet shrugs. "She decided it wasn't for her. She's started designing and selling her own jewelry, and she's doing very well."

Something clatters, and Jimmy snickers. Apparently, another fake piercing landed on his plate. It makes me grateful for my big inflatable suit.

"With my new, easier schedule, I'll definitely have time to help our unicorn with her bakery dreams," Scarlet says sweetly.

Marina lights up. "Is there news on that?"

"Not really," I reply. "Nonno will be away for a few days coming up, so Scarlet's going to help me spruce up Nonna's bakery while he's gone."

"That's a great idea," Gabi says. "Show him a new vision of what it could be."

I nod. "Exactly. New vision. New possibilities."

I have a picture in my mind of what I want, and I know Scarlet is the perfect person to make it a reality. When Nonno sees the bakery completely redone, he'll understand my vision. That's what I'm clinging to.

***

The next morning is filled with chaos and happy goodbyes as most of the house prepares to go back to real life. Sam and Bella are heading home to unpack and pack again for a trip to Hawaii. Jimmy and Beth are going to her place for a few days before she goes back to work. Rick, Ashley, Scarlet, Andrew, Icky, and I are all going back to San Francisco on the private jet. And of course, Max is staying with Zach and Marina for a few more days before he returns to San Diego.

I canceled my commercial flight home because of all the rules around flying with a furry person. I would have had to have him vaccinated with all kinds of paperwork. Of course, I plan to take him to the vet when we get home, but there are no such rules on private jets, and this was the easier path. Besides, Icky deserves a private jet. He should travel in style.

I roll my bags next to the bed, scoop Icky into my arms, and head downstairs. Thanks to all the extras I have for him, Marina had to loan me another suitcase, but I don't have to pay for bags on a private jet either. Score!

I follow the voices of my friends to the kitchen, where Max is sitting at the island trying in vain to eat one of my pumpkin spice muffins in peace.

"I promise to text you an update every time we talk," he tells Marina in a voice dripping with sarcasm.

She wraps an arm around his shoulders and gives him a shake.

"Sorry, bro. I just love you. I'm excited for you. I'll dial it down."

"I'm not sure you know how to do that," he says with a smirk. "But Gabi and I are talking through what this looks like after I go back to California. I think we can make this work for a while."

"Well, you can stay here whenever you want," Marina offers. "It doesn't matter where we are, the house is yours if you need it."

"Thank you, best sister in the world."

Marina laughs and comes my direction, holding her hands out.

"Let me hold little Icky baby while you grab your coffee," she says.

I hand him over and head to the coffee maker, pulling a mug down from the cabinet overhead. I laugh under my breath as she immediately begins talking to him in baby talk.

"Merry, these muffins are amazing," Bella tells me. "I'm on my third one and I kind of hate you for that."

I laugh out loud and pull up an empty stool at the huge kitchen island. I point to Marina.

"You can blame her. She's the one who had me here a day early so I could bake all the treats."

"Those spooky little pies last night were cute and delicious," Scarlet chimes in.

"And don't get me started on that beautiful cake you made for Jimmy and me this weekend," Beth says wistfully. "That was the sweetest thing to do. Thank you again."

I smile at my friends. "Wow, you guys. Thanks for all the love. Keep it coming. It doesn't get old."

I'm rewarded with a ripple of laughter, which is what I strive for in all things. As a rule, I think we should laugh more and worry less. We should allow ourselves to focus on hope and all the possibilities of the future. The dreary details of my current situation have muddied things for me for too long, and I find myself looking forward to going home and starting over.

Two hours later, I find myself standing on the tarmac in front of The Royal Rebels' private jet...holding a tiny black kitten in my hand and hugging Marina with my free arm.

"I'll see you next weekend, okay?" she says, giving Icky a little scritch under his chin.

"Definitely," I tell her. "Have fun and don't drive Max crazy."

She laughs and nods, then heads over to hug everyone else. Zach steps over to me.

"Doing alright, unicorn?"

"Doing just fine, Zach," I reply. "Thank you for this weekend. It was so much fun."

He grins at me, then looks over at Marina with pure love in his eyes.

"It was all the wifey," he says. "She just tells me what to do, and I do it. She has great vision."

I nod and hug him tight, then step back as two porters begin loading all our bags into the cargo hold. I bring Icky up to my face and rub his soft fur against my cheek, then plant a kiss on his little belly.

"Are you ready to go home, Icky?"

I slowly ascend the plane's steps, being careful to hold on to the rail as I go. I find a seat and wait for my friends to settle in. They chatter easily among themselves, and I turn my attention back to the furball in my hand, holding him up to the window.

"Say goodbye to New York, little man," I say quietly. "I'm taking you to the magical land of San Francisco. Big hills. Even bigger bridges.

You're gonna love it."

As if in reply, he lets out a monstrous yawn and follows it up with the tiniest squeak. I settle him in my lap as the pilot begins talking to our group. It's the standard seatbelt speech, and I make sure mine is fastened under Icky.

Before I know it, the aircraft door is closed and we're being pushed back from the terminal building. I look over at my friends and smile. Zach and Marina are becoming parents. Ashley and Rick bought a house, and they're about to get married. Scarlet's TV show just got renewed. Life suddenly feels ripe for change. Possibilities are about to bloom into reality. I can feel it.

It's time for me to put myself back out there again. I make a mental note to refresh my profiles on the dating apps I was using and to take a new picture. It's time to resume my search for my person. I say a silent prayer that my search won't be in vain. I believe he's out there, and I intend to find him.

The End

Want to see how Marina's brother Max's grand gesture paid off? Get Max & Gabi's exclusive first date scene free when you join my reader list. Click here!

One More to Go...

Merry's the last one standing.

All her friends have found their person. She's thrilled for them—really. But when a reckless driver nearly takes her out during a morning jog, the grumpy cop who shows up to take her statement isn't exactly making her feel warm and fuzzy.

Officer Nick Bright is all business. No small talk. No charm. Just facts, ma'am.

But Merry doesn't do grumpy. And when fate keeps throwing them together during the most magical time of year, she's determined to crack that scowl—even if it means ambushing him with Christmas cookies, an inflatable unicorn suit, and her relentless optimism.

He's grumpy. She's sunshine. This should be a disaster.

Turns out, Christmas miracles come in unexpected packages.

☞ **Start *Merry & Bright* now →**

Sneak Peek: Merry & Bright

Merry

"Explain it to me again," I ask my friend Scarlet, hoping to heaven she gets distracted and doesn't make me do this. Again.

She smirks at me. She's definitely onto me. Crud.

"It's good for you," she says, making sure to over-enunciate every syllable. Then she frowns.

"What?"

"I was going to say it gives you more energy, but you already have more than most people."

I roll my eyes. "Not true on multiple levels. First, I don't have more energy than most people, they're just too mired down by life to use it. Second, if it's supposed to give me energy why am I always so tired when I'm done?"

Laughter bubbles up out of Scarlet and she shakes her head at me.

"Can we just go jogging already? Do it for me if you won't do it for yourself. I don't want to go alone."

I give her the best side-eye in my arsenal. She knows my weakness: I'll do anything for my friends. I heave an intentionally over-dramatic sigh and push myself up off my couch.

"Fine," I say as I thump over to the entry of my tiny apartment and grab my sneakers. "But I get to decide the route."

"Oh, deal!"

She's way too excited about running on purpose. How is this my life?

Truth is, I've missed Scarlet. A ton. Out of our tight little group of four friends, Scarlet and I were the single girls. Our girlfriend Marina was the one we all thought would be the last of us to get married, but…nope. She was the first one. She didn't even want to date anyone and then boom. We got stuck in a traffic jam in the middle of the Golden Gate Bridge while she was dressed up like a mermaid and she met her man. That will forever be the weirdest story I tell.

Ashley wasn't looking to get involved with anyone either. In fact, she'd bite the head off any man who dared to approach her. She was on a firm dating hiatus, but our friend Rick was too perfect to resist. And he really is. Dude looks like a Viking god. Then Marina married Zach, and Rick proposed to Ashley, but Scarlet and I still had each other…until she met Andrew less than a year ago. Now I'm the spinster of the group and it doesn't feel awesome.

That wasn't the only big change for Scarlet, though. She's extremely busy, and not because of Andrew. She was filming the first season of her new TV show on the Home Network until October and, while we're all crazy proud of her, we've missed her so much. Her schedule is supposed to lighten up now but I haven't noticed much change yet. So, really, she could ask me to go bungee jumping and I'd do it because I'm just happy to spend time with her. Which means I'm going jogging.

I put my sneakers on, then grab a hair tie and my ID from my purse, because I'm always prepared. I pull my chestnut brown hair into a ponytail and slip the ID into the little pocket on my leggings and give Scarlet a double thumbs up.

"Ready, girl."

She doesn't move, she just stands there trying not to laugh.

"Are you really wearing that?"

I look down at myself as if I don't see the problem. I *do* see the problem, but it's not my problem. Last year, we all gave each other gag gifts for Christmas and I'm wearing mine. In our group of friends, I'm known as the unicorn because I'm always positive, full of energy, and sometimes a bit...extra. My gift was these super cool rainbow leggings with unicorns all over them, which I am currently wearing. Along with a hot pink t-shirt with a dancing cookie on it that says *Kiss Me I'm Delicious*.

"Yep, this is what I'm wearing," I say brightly, a crazed challenge flashing in my eyes. "Let's go."

I watch her expression closely. She's thinking about arguing but she knows she won't win. I will double-down so fast her head will spin. I'm not at all afraid to look ridiculous. It's just one of my many talents. Scarlet swallows hard.

"Okay, let's go!"

"Woohoo!"

We step out my door and head down the stairs, ending up in the back hallway of my grandfather's restaurant, Nonno's. It's too early for any of the kitchen staff to be doing lunch prep yet, so it's silent down here. And dark. It always creeps me out just a little bit when it's like this. Most people leave their apartment and they're outside. I leave mine and I'm inside an empty restaurant.

My grandparents moved out of the upstairs apartment years ago, opting to buy a house with more room. Over the years, various family members have used it. Thankfully, it was empty when I had the last of many fights with my wealthy parents over their need to control my life. So when I needed a place to stay because I couldn't handle them anymore, Nonno let me have the apartment.

We head straight out the back door and into the chilly San Francisco morning air. I lock the door and tuck my key into my leggings pocket.

"Okay, why running again? I'm just curious," I ask her as we begin stretching in the small parking lot behind Nonno's.

Scarlet thinks for a moment. "It helps me relax when there's too much I can't control. I get edgy and I hate it. Jogging helps me focus that energy on something else."

I frown at her. "I don't get it, but okay. When I'm frustrated, I bake delicious things."

Scarlet pulls her foot up behind her to stretch her quadricep muscle, then repeats the move on the other side.

"Well, then I guess I hope you're always frustrated," she jokes. "You're the best baker I know."

I laugh under my breath. I'm rarely frustrated because I refuse to spend time around things that frustrate me. I'm all about the good vibes. I can find the silver lining on the darkest cloud in the sky. The one and only exception is...Nonno.

He owns his restaurant and the small bakery next door that my Nonna used to run when she was alive. The two of them were inseparable and he adored her. When she passed, he shut down her bakery and refused to set foot inside. In the five years since, he's had either me or my cousins move various pieces of restaurant equipment or other supplies over there for storage. He won't even entertain the idea of re-opening Nonna's bakery. I always shared her love of a good cookie or a beautiful cake, yet Nonno won't even talk to me about it.

"Which way do you want to go?" Scarlet asks.

"We're wharf bound," I call out as I hit the sidewalk on Columbus Avenue at a somewhat gentle pace. From here, it's a straight shot down to Fisherman's Wharf. The bay breeze always lifts my spirits.

I don't want to admit it, but this probably *is* good for me. I'm on my feet a lot, whether I'm waitressing at Nonno's or spending time baking, but I rarely get any cardio. Going for a jog makes me feel like I'm doing something to stay healthy, which is probably important since I usually eat at least a few cookies every day. Throw the odd cupcake in there too. Occupational hazard.

We jog a few blocks in easy silence, then a red light stops us at the corner. I start up with lunges while we wait for the light to change.

"Any interesting dates lately?" Scarlet asks.

I briefly consider lying, but that serves no purpose. I wish I could share some good news with my friends, who all love me and want me to be happy, but since I decided to start dating again my life is a fruit salad of awkward encounters with unimpressive dudes. Not boys. Certainly not men. Just dudes.

"Unfortunately, no," I tell Scarlet. "It's like all the good men either married my friends or have left California entirely. Maybe I should move out of state. Didn't there used to be a plethora of burly, eligible, hot guys in Alaska? I feel like I remember reading an article or something."

Scarlet chuffs as the light changes and we jog into the crosswalk.

"You can't live in Alaska," she argues. "You'd curl up and die if you lived more than thirty miles from a Target."

I nearly trip over my own feet at the mere suggestion of living that far from my favorite store.

"Um...so would you. And they don't have Target in Alaska?"

Scarlet shakes her head. "Not where the big burly dudes live."

We run past a local coffee house and the smell of coffee tickles my nose, taunting me to float through the door and order an espresso and an almond croissant. That sounds so much better than talking about the barren desert my dating life has become.

"Well, it's not worth it then. Not even for a big, burly dude."

Scarlet giggles as we stop for another light.

"It's not a bad thing, really," I say. "I don't have to fight anyone for the remote. I can do whatever I want at any time."

Scarlet nods. "Valid points. Although, it's not like Andrew bosses me around. I can do whatever I want."

"I guarantee you he'd start telling you what to do if you came home and told him you were going to start fire juggling."

Scarlet laughs. "Well, I'll give you that."

"Then again, I do like the kissing that dating a decent guy can afford."

We take off as soon as the light turns green.

"No good candidates for kissing either?"

I stop jogging and put my hands on my hips.

"That is the sad state of affairs, my friend," I declare. "When I was much younger, sure, maybe some of these guys would be candidates for a good makeout session. But I've gotten to a point where I realize my kisses are valuable, you know? I'm not just giving away kisses to any guy. I want a guy who's worth it."

Scarlet watches me with compassion in her eyes, nodding.

"You'll find him, Mer. He's out there."

I nod and we start running again. Doubt creeps into my heart. My conviction was renewed when we came home from our trip to Sleepy Hollow last month, but now I'm starting to think it's just not going to happen for me.

"I'm not sure he is, Scarlet. I'm trying to be positive, but I also need to find a way to be okay with that. For my own peace of mind."

We jog around a couple pushing a baby stroller and something squeezes my heart. I want that. So bad. I don't need a ton of romance or drama or anything remotely resembling a Hallmark movie. I just want to meet a decent, kind man who wouldn't mind having a baby or five with me and living our lives in this city that I love so much.

"Why don't we focus on the bakery project while I'm in town? It'll give you something else to think about."

I manage a smile, but I'm not sure it's a good idea. Nonno has a trip coming up, and it would be perfect timing to surprise him by upgrading the space where the bakery was. Truth is, I'm feeling a little fragile lately, and getting serious about pursuing my last ditch effort to convince Nonno to finally let me open Nonna's old bakery...that's scary. What if that goes wrong too?

He's been saying no for years. First it was because I didn't have enough experience baking, so I turned the foyer of the restaurant into a grab and go bakery that has been highly successful. Then it was no because there wasn't space in Nonna's old bakery. He's been shoving old busted restaurant equipment back there for years. All of my offers to clean it up are refused. He keeps saying he needs the space, but he doesn't.

Anyway, clinging to the hope of changing his mind someday is all I really have right now. If I play my final card and he still says no, I'm not sure I can deal with that rejection. I don't even want to think about it.

"I might want to wait on that," I hedge as we jog through the next block. "Feels like it might not be the time."

I don't miss Scarlet giving me the side-eye, but I ignore it. I appreciate that she's concerned. If the tables were turned, I would be too. I just can't face it right now. Final answer.

Maybe.

The first whiff of fresh, salty air hits my nose as we near Fisherman's Wharf. It's my favorite part of the city, and my spirits lift just knowing that we'll soon be strolling along Pier 39 and taking a break on my favorite bench where I can watch the sea lions barking at each other. They just lay there in the sun, fat and happy. What can I say...I'm a simple girl.

Traffic is noticeably busier in this part of the city as tourists begin to intermingle with regular city traffic. We stop at another corner and wait for the light. Car horns begin blaring as people grow impatient with each other.

"I know you're trying to help," I tell her. "And I love you for it, but I feel like I shouldn't disturb the fragile peace in my life right now, you know?"

Scarlet nods, her eyes full of understanding, as the light changes and we continue jogging down Columbus towards the wharf. I try to relax and focus on the scents of the wharf and the sight of the bay ahead of us, but there's a guy in a lime green SUV that keeps honking his horn. Obnoxiously. I look over to see what he looks like and he's red-faced and shaking his head impatiently. Calm down, dude.

By the time we're on the last block before the wharf, I'm laughing at the guy. Traffic is so bad right now Scarlet and I are actually getting farther faster than the cars. We wait for the last light to change and jog up the sidewalk while he's stuck waiting for traffic to move.

We round the corner and continue down the sidewalk, jogging up a few smaller streets until we're jogging down Jefferson towards Pier 39. Somehow, lime green SUV dude comes sailing up the street. He's leaning on his horn, weaving in and out of cars by driving up on the sidewalk when he can't find another way.

"That guy's crazy," Scarlet says while we wait for another light. "It's three weeks till Christmas…who can be that angry? What a jerk!"

I smirk. "I guarantee you I've either already been on a date with him or he's going to send me a message on the Love in the Bay app. This is exactly the kind of jerk who'd want to go out with me."

"You know what? We're going to manifest your Mr. Right," Scarlet says. "You're gonna meet him today."

I snort laugh and shake my head. "You're just saying that because you don't know how bad it is out there, Scarlet. It's bad."

The light is still red and she starts running around me in a circle, waving jazz hands all over me, chanting.

"Mr. Right, Mr. Right, Mr. Right today…hey!"

I laugh out loud. "What are you doing?"

"I just manifested your dream guy," she says with ridiculous confidence. "You'll meet him today. You're welcome."

I laugh again, giving her a gentle shove and she giggles.

"Laugh all you want, unicorn girl. It's gonna happen."

The light turns green. Finally. We jog down to The Embarcardo and my spirits lighten instantly. I love this area because the sidewalk widens into a much bigger space. It's pretty crowded on the weekends, but it's nice this afternoon. Except for the traffic, of course. I can still hear the lime green SUV's horn honking.

Construction cones are everywhere out here, blocking off an entire lane. We stop and jog in place not far from the corner we just turned. When we realize there's no space for pedestrians to cross safely, we both stop jogging and gawk at the chaos.

"Well, this is stupid," Scarlet mutters.

I step out closer to the curb to see whether there's a crosswalk anywhere we can get to, and that's when I hear the horn. Right behind me. Everything happens in slow motion.

I turn just in time to see that same lime green SUV barreling up the street. He's driving half on the sidewalk so he can go around the other cars and he's talking on his cell phone. He doesn't see me.

I scream, and Scarlet yanks me away as hard as she can. Something in my ankle twists and a sharp pain shoots fiery streaks up my leg. I scream again as we both fall and hit the building next to us, and the SUV slams into a light pole on the corner just a few feet away from us. The sound of screeching tires and crunching metal is deafening.

Shaking like a leaf, I wrap my arms around Scarlet...who landed on top of me.

"Are you okay?" I croak out. "Scarlet?"

She rolls off of me with a groan. A few good Samaritans rush over to help. Some guys are yanking at the car door on the SUV, and a woman rushes over to us.

"I'm a nurse," she says with calm authority. "Are you hurt?"

I look over at Scarlet and she nods gingerly, muttering that she's okay. I look at the nurse.

"I think we're okay, maybe check the guy in the car first."

She nods and disappears. Another lady squats in front of us.

"We called 9-1-1 so just try and stay calm," she says.

"Merry, you're bleeding," Scarlet says.

She points to my forehead and I raise my fingers to the spot. Yep. She's right.

I scoot back enough, using my good leg, so I can lean against the building. The only pain I feel is in my ankle. My head feels okay. I think I just scratched my forehead when we landed.

"I'm okay," I tell her. "Are you? Oh my gosh…"

"I'm okay," she says, scooting over to me and grabbing my hand.

Sirens wail in the distance, getting closer and closer. I try to take deep, calming breaths but the shock of what's happened seems to be taking over. I try to turn my ankle and end up crying out in pain.

"Don't move it," Scarlet says softly, giving my hand a squeeze. "Don't move anything if you don't have to."

I nod. Waiting for someone to come and help me only seems to make me panic more. I look over to the twisted wreck of the SUV just in time to see two men pulling the door free. The red-faced driver climbs out. There's some kind of scuffle, but I can't see everything happening. I turn my head towards Scarlet.

"If that's the guy you manifested for me, I have complaints."

She tries to fight it, but I see the smile twitching at the corners of her mouth. I grin at her and let out a little laugh as I lean my head back against the wall.

The nurse comes back to us and kneels down next to me, taking my wrist in her hand.

"I'm just checking your pulse, okay?"

I nod. My ankle is really starting to hurt. My knee doesn't feel so great either, now that I think of it.

"How hard did you hit your head?" she asks, nodding at my forehead.

"Not hard," I tell her. "I think I just scraped it when we landed on the ground."

"I'm Karen, by the way," she says calmly. "Can you follow my finger with just your eyes?"

I do as she asks, and she seems pleased with the result. She looks at Scarlet.

"How about you?"

Scarlet nods. "I'm okay. I scraped my elbow, that's all."

"Is the driver okay?" I ask Karen, prompting a laugh.

"He's okay right now," she says dryly. "He won't be for long. He tried to flee the scene."

"Nooo!" I gasp. Wow. He really is a jerk.

Two police cars, an ambulance, and a fire truck converge on the scene within seconds of each other.

"Oh, good," Scarlet says. "It's not Engine 14 or I'd have to text Andrew before he ended up in a panic."

I smile at her. "Maybe you manifested one of them for me. Why should you be the only one who marries a fireman?"

Karen smiles at me. "Now that's the kind of thing I like to hear. If you're joking, that's a really good sign."

"Oh, you want jokes, Karen? I'll just tell you about my social life."

Scarlet and I bust out laughing, and soon Karen does as well. I also start crying a little, which I don't expect. Karen pats me on the hand.

"It's okay. That's normal. You've had a shock."

I nod. "Thank you. Thank you for stopping to help."

She smiles at me, then two EMTs rush over and she steps back. I'm vaguely aware of her telling them about my pulse and my head. I just keep leaning back against the wall and try to calm down.

Someone puts a blood pressure cuff around my arm and I close my eyes, focusing on my breath and trying to steady myself.

"...BP's a little high..."

"...I've got him, can you stay with the victims?"

"...are those unicorns?"

I open my eyes to find a blonde EMT smiling at me.

"Hey there, I'm Kelly," she says, then she nods to my other side where there's a very muscled-up blonde policeman. "This is Officer Bright. What's your name?"

"Merry."

"Good to meet you, Merry, how hard did you hit your head?"

"I barely scraped it when I fell. My ankle really hurts."

She nods. Her colleagues are rushing around behind her and over by the wreck. One is kneeling down by Scarlet to check her out. Officer Bright is kneeling on my other side, wearing mirrored sunglasses and looking like he'd rather be anywhere but next to a woman wearing unicorn leggings. He looks...familiar.

Kelly moves down to my ankle and frowns.

"I'm going to check this, Merry. It may hurt a little."

I nod and watch as she gently turns my foot just slightly. A sharp pain launches like a rocket through my ankle. I yelp and jolt hard, flailing my right arm and managing to hit Officer Bright right in the face. His sunglasses go flying over his shoulder as I grab his arm on impulse and squeeze. Muscles tense in response and I let go immediately, offering him what I'm sure is a winning combo of a grimace and an apologetic smile.

"I'm so sorry," I say to him as Kelly says the exact same thing to me.

I watch sheepishly as another officer retrieves the sunglasses and hands them back to him. Officer Bright tucks them into his uniform shirt pocket, then turns his incredibly gorgeous ice blue eyes on me.

Wow.

Wow, wow, wow.

"Holy c—"

"Can we get her on a stretcher so I can really have a look at that ankle?"

A stretcher magically appears, courtesy of two EMTs, but they run back over to the wreck. Kelly nods at the officer and he bends down and scoops me up in one quick move, gently setting me down on the stretcher.

"Whoa! Uh...thank you."

The corner of his mouth twitches into a half smile.

He definitely looks familiar to me. I watch him as he stands off to the side, keeping an eye on the scene and jumping in when he's needed. I've seen this guy before. I know I have.

Scarlet leans over. "Looks familiar, huh?"

I nod. "I've seen him before."

"Yep. We have."

I turn my head to Scarlet. "Where?"

"Think back to a certain traffic jam on a certain bridge with a certain friend of ours who was dressed like a mermaid..."

I gasp out loud. And then, to my horror, I point right at him.

"Officer Honey Badger!"

Kelly laughs, but keeps it together. I immediately regret doing that. He scowls at me and puts the sunglasses back on. A muscle feathers in his perfect looking, strong jaw. I look over at Scarlet.

"Oh my gosh, he's the cop who told us we could get out of the car and stretch when we were stuck on the bridge, right?"

She nods. "And I'm pretty sure you flirted with him."

The realization hits me. "Oh yeah! And he wasn't feeling it at all. He just stood there, not smiling. No reaction. One of my finer moments."

Scarlet giggles. "You seem okay. You really didn't hit your head?"

I shake my head. "Nope. My ankle is twisted, that's all. And now my pride because I'm reliving the rejection."

She laughs under her breath and pulls out her phone. "I'm going to see if I can get one of the girls to pick us up."

"Okay, remember Marina isn't home yet."

Scarlet nods and steps away. Marina and Zach are returning home today from a quick trip to visit his family in the U.K. They don't land until this evening. Scarlet wanders away, leaving me with Kelly and the Honey Badger.

"I don't think it's broken, but you should have it checked out," Kelly tells me. "Lay back and let me have a look at that forehead."

I lay back on the stretcher as Kelly checks my eyes with a small light, then pokes around on my forehead.

"There's no bruising or swelling," she says, then she wanders back to the ambulance for something. And now I'm alone on a stretcher next to the very silent Officer Honey Badger.

I study his face. He kind of looks like he wants to kill me. He probably could...with just his thumb. There's a lot of muscles going on over there. It's funny, since he seems one thousand percent immune to my charms, it's kind of shocking we haven't been marked as a connection by one of the dating apps I use. That seems to be all the universe needs to send me on another horrible date.

Actually, he's pretty handsome. And muscley. And his eyes are so pretty. He's married. That's what it is. Married with thirteen kids. But dang...that jawline of his is a thing of beauty.

All of a sudden my mouth goes completely dry, and yet my throat does some kind of weird half swallow, half twitch, which causes me to cough uncontrollably. I look away and sit up. He steps forward and puts a hand on my arm.

"Ma'am, you should lie down."

I lean over, coughing more, struggling to control it, and cursing the universe at making me feel like I'm failing life right now. I just choked on my own spit in front of the hottest guy I've ever seen in my life. So that's good. I'll overthink about this until the end of my days.

I get myself under control and croak out, "Don't call me ma'am."

Something cold hits my ankle and I look over to find Kelly pressing an ice pack against it. I smile my thanks as another EMT comes to stand in front of me.

"We'll transport you to Mercy General for x-rays."

I shake my head emphatically. "Nope. I'm not going to the hospital, thanks."

All heads turn to me, including the super handsome one.

"What?" he blurts.

I glance between him and the EMTs and shake my head again.

"I can't afford a hospital bill," I explain. "Or an ambulance bill. Not going."

I look around for Scarlet, who is still on her phone and wandering away again.

"That's not a good idea, ma'am," Officer Honey Badger says.

I hold a finger up to scold him. "I'm not kidding. Stop calling me ma'am. Please. I won't be thirty for three more weeks. My name is Merry."

That seems to put the misguided yet very handsome police officer in his place.

"Your ankle should be checked for breaks," Kelly asserts.

I scoff. "I've broken a bone or two in my time. It's not broken, and if it's still hurting me on Monday I'll call my regular doctor."

Kelly frowns. "I really advise against this. You should be checked out."

I nod. "I will be. By my own doctor."

The EMTs and Officer Honey Badger all stare at me as if I've lost my mind.

"Look, I appreciate the concern, but we all know you can't make me go for something like this. I'll be fine."

The EMT next to Kelly shakes his head in disbelief.

"Okay, I'll need you to sign a waiver."

I grin up at him. "Gladly."

"Ma'am, I—"

I grumble out loud and turn to the cop again.

"Seriously, I don't care how many muscles you're carrying around under that uniform, you have to stop calling me that. Now."

Everyone grows silent. Embarrassment coils in my gut as I watch the EMT wander off to find the waiver and Kelly eyes me with a weird combination of delight and concern. I can't look at the cop. I put my hand up to shield my face so he can't see me either.

"Keep it elevated and iced all day today," Kelly tells me. "Try to stay off of it all weekend. And if there's any redness or if the pain increases please go to an emergency room."

I nod again. "I promise. And thank you."

She gives me a parting smile and heads back to the ambulance as her colleague leans over me with a clipboard and a pen. I take them from him and sign where he tells me, then hand them back quickly.

"Thank you again."

He nods. "I need my gurney back now."

I look around me for a bench or anything to sit on while Scarlet finds us a ride. There's nothing. Great. I move to get down off the stretcher and Officer Honey Badger puts his hand up to stop me.

"Wait a minute," he says firmly. "Where do you plan to go? You can't walk on that ankle."

"You don't need to worry about me, Officer," I tell him with a smile. I ignore his hand and slide off the stretcher anyway, standing on my good foot. "My friend is finding us a ride."

Scarlet steps over with perfect timing, grumbling under her breath.

"I can't get Ashley on the phone, and Andrew has a test at work today. He told me his phone would be off during that time," she says. "And no one else can help."

An awkward silence settles like a giant womp womp. Gingerly, I adjust my stance when my good ankle starts to get wobbly.

"Let's just get a rideshare," I tell her.

"No."

Both Scarlet and I look at Officer Honey Badger like he's grown a second head. I shift anxiously.

"I'm sorry?"

He shakes his head at me.

"I can't let you get in a rideshare with a stranger," he grumbles. "That's not safe."

I laugh softly, then stop suddenly when I realize he's not joking. In fact, he looks so serious I wonder if he ever laughs.

"They all go through background checks," I remind him.

He shakes his head again.

"No offense, ma'am, but—"

"Merry," I say in a clipped tone. "My name is Merry. I'll give you fifty bucks to stop calling me ma'am, okay? What's it gonna take?"

It's hard to gauge his expression with his sunglasses back in place, but I notice the tiniest little twitch at the corner of his mouth. He nods solemnly.

"Okay, Merry," he says calmly, making me smile unexpectedly at the sound of my name on his lips. "Are you ready to go or would you like to wobble around on the sidewalk some more?"

I smirk at him. "I'm fine with the rideshare. But thank you. For finally calling me Merry."

That muscle ticks in his jaw again.

"You're not taking a rideshare," he says with quiet authority.

Scarlet huffs at my side.

"Merry, this is faster than waiting for a rideshare," she says. "Let's get you home so you can put your ankle up and get some fresh ice."

I scowl at the police officer, and he flashes me a perfect smile that's just dripping with sarcasm.

"C'mon," he says, and before I have a second to object he scoops me up in his arms and stands.

"Wow!" Scarlet exclaims as I'm carried off to his squad car.

She rushes to follow. I look down at the name badge on his uniform.

N. Bright

"What's the N stand for?"

I catch him suppressing a smile again.

"You can call me Officer Bright."

"Hmm..does it stand for...No Longer Calling Me Ma'am?"

I'm rewarded with a half smile.

"Yep."

Scarlet runs over and opens the back passenger door of the squad car. He bends over and gently places me on the seat, then pulls away and closes the door before I can make more guesses. Scarlet gets in from the other side and offers me a mischievous grin.

"Can I manifest or what?" she whispers proudly.

I shake my head in confusion. "What?"

She points to the officer, who is standing just outside the car doing who knows what.

"Officer Bright sounds very close to Mr. Right," she says brightly. "I'm calling this done, my friend. He's your person."

📖 *Ready to curl up with one last romance?*

There's one final story waiting in the San Francisco Hearts series.

Merry & Bright is a feel-good, grumpy-sunshine Christmas romance best enjoyed with hot cocoa, twinkle lights, and a soft blanket.

☞ **Read *Merry & Bright* now**

About the Author

~❦~

Dianne Oren writes sweet rom coms and lives in Texas with her husband, crazy doggos Duke & Daisy, Finn the cat, and an 8 pound murder muffin named Rebel. She loves embroidery, travel, and is completely addicted to iced coffee.

You can connect with me on:
🌐 https://dianneoren.com
f https://www.facebook.com/DianneOrenOfficial

Subscribe to my newsletter:
✉ https://dianneoren.com/subscribe

Also by Dianne Oren

How to Date a Mermaid

Marina has spent her entire life swimming against the current—and she's finally close to the future she's worked so hard to earn. A job at the city's most prestigious law firm is her first step toward law school, where she plans to fight for kids in crisis just like she once was. One slip-up could cost her everything, and her notoriously strict boss doesn't tolerate distractions—or bad press.

So of course, the one spontaneous moment Marina allows herself lands her in a viral video with a world-famous rock star...while she's dressed as a mermaid and singing in public.

Determined to protect her future, Marina plans to disappear—until her meddling friend tells Zach exactly where to find her. When he shows up at the library where she's singing to children and curious onlookers start pulling out their phones, the two are forced into a hasty escape. One impromptu dinner later, Marina finds herself agreeing to the one thing she swore she wouldn't risk: dating him in secret.

Zach promises to protect her identity. But the more time they steal together, the harder it becomes to keep their worlds separate—and the harder it is for Marina to ignore the truth. She's not just hiding from the media; she's hiding from a future that scares her more than any viral video—one where she lets someone in.

With her carefully planned future on the line and her guarded heart opening against her will, Marina must decide whether to keep chasing the life she planned...or take a leap toward the love she never expected.

Fake It Till You Make It
Ashley

My ex-fiancé jilted me twice—proof my taste in men is deeply questionable. So I'm done with relationships. Permanently.

Just call me the Dragon Lady. I guard my heart like a dragon guards treasure. Unfortunately, when the jerk shows up again, I need proof I've moved on. Fast.

Enter Rick: six-foot-two, absurdly attractive, and the sole surviving resident of my friend zone. One fake Valentine's date. No feelings. Definitely no complications.

Except we're also best man and maid of honor at our best friends' wedding. And pretending is getting harder than I expected.

Rick

Ashley thinks I'm safely tucked in the friend zone. She's wrong.

I've never been passive about what I want—and what I want is *her*. Agreeing to be her fake date isn't a favor. It's strategy.

When she accidentally face-plants her strawberry mask onto my white shirt? I keep it. Wear it as pajamas just to mess with her. She calls it The Great Ashley Shirt War. I call it phase one.

She thinks I'm patient. She has no idea I'm playing the long game.

And I always win.

Running to the Rescue
Scarlet

I have six weeks to win the Home Network's Decorator's Showcase and the $250,000 grand prize. I've entered this contest three years running. This year, I'm living in an abandoned warehouse in a sketchy neighborhood just to make it happen.

I don't do distractions. I don't do spontaneous. I schedule everything—including my love life.

So when I meet Andrew, a firefighter with an annoyingly perfect smile, I feel the attraction. But I shut it down immediately. I ask him if he'd like to have coffee. In six weeks. When the contest is over.

He laughs. Says he'll wait.

Then a fire destroys my project three weeks before the deadline.

Andrew is the one who pulls me from the blaze. A news photographer catches the moment—my face lit by flames, half-covered in ash, Andrew carrying me out. The headline: "The Phoenix and the Fireman."

I tell everyone I'm done. There's no time to start over.

Andrew—and my meddling friends—disagree. They replace my equipment, rally support, and offer up the fire station as my new location. I can redesign their kitchen and living room. It's perfect. It's also impossible to keep things professional when Andrew is there. Every. Single. Day.

Andrew

I used to be like Scarlet—career-obsessed, scheduling life down to the minute. Then I lost a friend. He died while I was too busy climbing ladders to pick up the phone.

I won't make that mistake again.

When Scarlet asks me out for coffee in six weeks, I know exactly what she's doing. Putting life on hold for ambition. I've been there. It doesn't end well.

Then I pull her from a fire and everything changes.

She wants to give up. I won't let her. My crew and I offer her the fire station, and she throws herself into the rebuild with the same relentless focus that's going to burn her out.

I'm not backing off. She asked for six weeks. I'm giving her every reason to change her mind.

Merry & Bright
Merry

A runaway car. A twisted ankle. A very serious police officer who keeps calling me ma'am.

I'm turning thirty—not eighty—and Officer Nicholas Bright is not amused by my objections. He's buttoned-up, stoic, and completely unprepared for my nonstop commentary...until I finally make him laugh.

He insists on driving me home.
Then he keeps showing up.
"Just checking in."

I'm a baker—specifically, a Christmas-cookie maximalist. When Nick mentions that his adopted grandmother used to bake with him every Christmas, something shifts. She has Alzheimer's now. Most days, she doesn't remember him at all.

So I suggest cookie decorating.

And somehow, I end up going with him.

Nick

I don't believe in optimism. Life cured me of that.

Merry is sunshine and chaos—too cheerful, too talkative, and far too determined to see past my badge and dark sunglasses. I tell myself we're just friends. I have nothing to offer her. My grandmother is slipping away, and Christmas—her favorite season—feels like salt in an open wound.

Then Merry comes with me to the care home to decorate cookies. And for a few precious minutes, my grandmother remembers me.

I break every boundary I built. I don't care anymore.

I want Merry. And I want more than friendship. For the first time, I'm willing to risk my heart to get it.